COME HOME TO DEATH

Come Home to Death

A Patrick Dawlish Mystery

John Creasey *writing as* Gordon Ashe

OPEN ROAD

INTEGRATED MEDIA
NEW YORK

Copyright © 1958 by John Creasey

ISBN: 978-1-5040-9819-9

This edition published in 2025 by Open Road Integrated Media, Inc.
180 Maiden Lane
New York, NY 10038
www.openroadmedia.com

COME HOME TO DEATH

1

FRIGHTENED GIRL

She was frightened when she came to see Dawlish, and younger than he expected; not more than twenty-two or three. Without her fear, she might have been pretty; with it, she was all eyes and unsteady lips. She had one of those deceptive-looking figures, but hid her small waist with an ill-fitting twin set, an uneasy combination of grey and green. Where the cardigan opened, at the two top buttons, the tight-fitting jumper clung to her breasts and showed what her figure was really like.

She had a quality of persistence, too, for she had written to Dawlish twice, and telephoned three times; invariably he had said that he was sorry, he couldn't help her. Nor could he help her now, although he suspected that his wife, Felicity, felt much the same as he: that it was a pity they were on the point of going away. For Marion Ard really looked as if she was in trouble, and had no one else to turn to.

'You see,' she said, clasping her hands tightly in front of her, 'it's all so tenuous. I can't offer the police any proof that what I say is really happening. They think they're dealing with a neurotic case, but I'm not neurotic; this man does follow me everywhere I go.'

Felicity glanced out of the window of the drawing-room at the Dawlishs' country-home. Beyond was the garden, the drive between tall, grass-clad banks, the tall trees and the flowering shrubs, in full leaf now, for this was early summer. Beyond were the rolling fields of Surrey, and, in the distance, wooded land. It was quiet and beautiful, and even the sounds of the country were muted.

No one was in sight outside.

'Oh, I know exactly what you think,' Marion said, and jumped up, nearly upsetting her cup, which was half full of tea. 'You think I'm the only one who sees this man; that it's an hallucination. But it's *not*, I swear it isn't.'

Felicity Dawlish, carrying her forty years lightly, wished that the girl had not made that obviously dramatic movement.

'Miss Ard,' said Dawlish, who was standing massively in the window, holding his cup and saucer in one hand, and a plate of sticky, cream cakes in the other, 'there isn't anyone outside now.'

'He never follows me to the police, or if I'm going for help,' she said.

'Could he have known that you were coming to see me?'

The visitor turned away and stared across the countryside, to a distant farmhouse which showed vaguely, a reddish brown. Felicity looked at her husband and shook her head, as if to say 'don't drive her too far'. Dawlish, a clear foot taller than the girl, and dressed in bulky Harris tweeds for an English summer, looked at the back of her head and wrinkled his broken nose, as if he were not sure what to think of her. Her shoulders were bowed, as if she were crying—or praying.

'I don't know what he knows about me,' she whispered at last. 'I only know that it's driving me mad. I can't go on being frightened much longer, I really can't.' She turned on Dawlish almost savagely, and the anger in her brown eyes startled both him and his wife. 'Why don't you help me? You're supposed to be so clever, you're supposed to be so brave. Why *don't* you? Is it just because I haven't enough money? I've this'—she snatched at a brooch pinned loosely to the loose weave of the jumper—'and this and this.' She tugged at a tiny solitaire diamond ring, and a gold signet ring. 'And this and this and this!' She pulled her ear-rings off, so roughly that it must have hurt, and then opened her large handbag and took out a small black purse. She held all these in her hands and thrust them towards him; and her cupped hands were trembling, as her lips were quivering. 'That's everything I've got. Isn't it enough?'

Felicity looked acutely distressed, but there was little change in Dawlish's voice or expression; a new note of gentleness, that was all.

'It isn't a question of money,' he said. 'It's just that I won't be here.'

'You could stay and help me if you wanted to!'

How did one refuse her, in such a way that she would give up trying?

Dawlish caught Felicity's eye, and knew that she was almost wavering; but they must not waver. They were going away for two months: Felicity to rest and recuperate after a grave operation, Dawlish to be with her. This was a holiday which they had promised each other for years, and Felicity's need made it much more than a holiday. Their ship was due to sail next morning from Southampton; they were to get up at five, to drive to the port. Everything was planned, most was paid for; and this girl with her private hauntings was nothing at all to them. She had not even been sent by a friend or a friend of a friend. When she had first telephoned, she had said that she had got Dawlish's name out of a newspaper article, and so was positive he would help.

'Miss Ard,' said Dawlish, even more gently, 'we're leaving here at six in the morning. The house will be closed up after tomorrow night, even the servants will be away. There's nothing I can do in the time. I'm really sorry.'

'Sorry,' she echoed, in a choky voice. 'That's what everyone says. I'm sorry, sorry, sorry! What will you say when I'm dead?'

Dawlish could not find a word to answer that. The girl glared at him with those beautiful burning eyes, trembling hands still holding her trinkets and her purse. Outside, clear through the open windows, were the pleasing country sights and the soft country sounds, and here was the girl's fear and her heavy breathing, no other noise at all.

Felicity broke the silence, almost with a sigh.

'You've a few hours today, Pat. Could you give Miss Ard some advice on the best thing to do?'

The hope which was born in the girl's eyes made it quite impossible for Dawlish to say no, but Felicity, having committed him, averted her eyes hastily, and picked up her cup. The girl stood willing Dawlish to help, with the treasures in her hands, for she did not know that the decision had already been made.

'I'm not very hopeful,' Dawlish said, 'but I'll try.'

First there was unbelief; then a show of tears, then near humility.

'Oh, I knew you would,' Marion Ard said, very huskily. 'I couldn't believe you'd refuse, not after what I've read about you. Mrs Dawlish, I can't tell you how grateful I am, I really can't tell you. I'll never be able to say thank you properly. If only Mr Dawlish would follow me, if only he would see for himself that someone does come after me, and would tell the police about it. I'm sure that would be enough, they'd listen to him, like they always do.'

It was pointless to tell her that the newspaper article exaggerated his reputation, and that the police were not at all eager for his advice; pointless to tell her that the years had mellowed him, and that he no longer did those wilder things for which the newspapers had made him famous. Apart from anything else, Felicity's illness had frightened him; the time had come to consider her more than his own whims and fancies; more than the once compulsive urge to investigate any crime that came his way. Now he could look back at some of the things he had done, and some of the desperate chances he had taken, and marvel at them as a man would marvel at the folly of his youth.

But youth was not really far away, and this girl could make it seem very close. He wanted to help her; only loyalty to Felicity and the call of the ship had made him fight against the desire.

Felicity, not the girl, had caused the breach.

'I'll try to help you,' he promised, 'and I'll see some friends of mine in London, they might be able to help a little, too.'

Slowly, Marion put the trinkets down; as slowly, she turned towards Felicity. There were tears in her eyes; in its way this moment could not have been more touching. She put her arms round Felicity in a strangely daughter-to-mother way, and hugged her, without saying another word.

Felicity looked up at Dawlish.

Dawlish said: 'Hm-hm. What time is it?' He knew very well that it was twenty minutes past four. 'Miss Ard, there are one or two things I must arrange with my wife; will you forgive me if we leave you here for ten minutes? Then I'd like you to head for the station, and I'll follow at a distance.'

'Of course I don't mind! I'm only so grateful. I don't mind at all.'

The difficulty, once Dawlish was alone with Felicity, was to take the girl and the situation really seriously, to realise that he was now committed to leaving Felicity here on her own for this last evening. Felicity leaned against the kitchen sink, and Dawlish stood by the Formica-topped table, his head a little on one side, and his big jaw thrust forward.

'Ten minutes before she arrived you were saying how impossible it was to be ready unless I dropped everything in the garden and weighed in with the packing. Remember?'

'I'll manage, darling.' Felicity's eyes were bright.

'This morning when you read her letter you said that nothing in this world would make you agree even to my seeing her.'

'Well, I didn't think she'd come here, did I?' asked Felicity, and went on more briskly: 'It isn't any use wasting time now.'

'If I'm back before midnight I'll be lucky,' Dawlish said. 'As soon as I've gone, ring Tim, and ask him to meet me at the station, will you? I might be able to push this job on to him, but I doubt it.'

'If there seems to be any real cause for her fears you simply must make the police help,' said Felicity, as if that was simply up to Dawlish. 'But I'll ring Tim.' She looked at him very thoughtfully as she went on: 'What do you think of her, Pat?'

'I think she thinks she's being followed by a man wherever she goes, and that she thinks he wants to kill her.'

'Yes, but do you think he exists?'

'With luck, I'll know before the night's out,' said Dawlish, more briskly. 'Sweet, the labels aren't done for the baggage yet. I was going to do them this evening. I haven't jotted down those notes for Old Josh to have for the garden. I haven't—'

'I'll do everything. You just think about the girl.'

'I've known a time when you would have contemplated divorce proceedings if I worried about one with half her looks.' But Dawlish smiled, and that made him remarkably handsome; it was almost possible to forget the broken bridge of his nose. The sun shining through the kitchen window caught the top of his corn-coloured hair, and lit up the strength of his features and the cornflower blue of his eyes. He was a blond giant, and quite as strong as he looked. 'Second thoughts, sweet. Telephone Ted as well as Tim, and one of the others if he's out. Have two at Victoria Station if possible—one for certain. There's just a chance that the man does exist and know that she's been here for help, so he'd try to make sure I didn't see him. Ask Tim or whoever decides to help to see if anyone follows me.'

'Yes, dear,' said Felicity.

She did not say what was in her mind; that she knew from all the signs that his thoughts were already far away from her and the problem of packing and preparing for the trip; they were centred exclusively on the girl. Here was a case which she would never be able to hold against him.

'Try not to be back later than ten.' She added: 'I'll have everything ready by then.'

No one followed the girl from Dawlish's house, Four Ways, when a taxi took her to Haslemere Station, only a few miles away.

She travelled third class and Dawlish first, but no man took any notice of her, as far as he could tell.

He saw his friend Tim Jeremy at Victoria, a tall man who was thin enough to look gaunt. Dawlish gave no sign of recognition, and was quite sure that if a man followed him or the girl, Tim would not fail to notice it. No one else he knew was in sight.

He saw Tim again in Harven Street, where Marion Ard had a flat; and he saw Tim shake his head, which meant that he had seen no one who showed any interest in Dawlish or in the girl.

The house was one of a long, uninteresting terrace, and her flat was at the front of the second floor. The hall and staircase were in good repair, but this part of Kensington was comparatively cheap; there was no hint of luxury anywhere. She opened the door of her flat with a Yale key, and then stood back; and again he saw an expression akin to fear on her pert face.

'Will you—will you go in first?' she asked. 'I'm always afraid that he'll be waiting for me, I hate coming into the flat.'

She touched him with an odd feeling of danger, so that Dawlish moved swiftly once he was inside. But no one was in the small living-room, with its two armchairs, its corner sink and gas-stove, its little shelf of books, the carpet which was wearing thin. There was no one in the tiny bedroom, which had just room for a divan bed, and a small table with a mirror on it. At least everything looked fresh and clean. Marion Ard was houseproud enough to have pleased Felicity.

'There's no one here,' Dawlish assured her, and she came in quickly, and closed the door.

'I know you think I'm mad, like all of them,' she said, 'but you won't, when I've shown you these photographs. I've taken four in all, and they've all been of the same man standing across the street, watching. The camera doesn't lie, does it?' She began to rummage in a box, then drew back and went on: 'I could have sworn I'd put them there. I took them out to show the police yesterday, and took them to Scotland Yard, but—well they just wouldn't take notice of me, that's why I came to you. I meant to have them with me today, but I never seem to remember anything.' She stopped rummaging, and looked at him with a puzzled expression clouding her eyes. He did not know what to make of her, and somehow he was not so well impressed now as he had been at Four Ways. It was as if she was fooling him, and hoped that he hadn't noticed.

'What do you think they want of you?' he asked.

'I don't know; if I did it would be much better,' Marion said. 'The worst part of it is the mystery—*why* do they haunt me so? Sometimes I think they're just trying to drive me crazy.' She was searching through her handbag, but could not find the snap-shots. 'I *can't* have lost them,' she said abruptly, and he saw the nervous tension with which she began to search again.

She found nothing.

She stopped at last, turned away, and dropped on to an easy chair, staring helplessly, hopelessly; she seemed more pathetic because she didn't speak, and the unfavourable impression faded.

'You've probably mislaid them,' Dawlish said. But now he was quite sure that she was a little odd, and probably suffering from a persecution mania; but it would not help to tell her so. 'Is there anything else you'd like to show me while I'm here?'

'I—I wanted to show you the photographs,' she said, drearily. 'And I wanted to show you where the man always stands.'

'Then show me.'

'If I haven't the photographs you won't believe me.' She didn't stir from her chair.

'What I'm going to do is to arrange for friends of mine to watch you and this house day and night for the next few days,' Dawlish said. 'They'll do it so discreetly that you won't even know that it's being watched yourself. So that, at the end of a week, they'll have a clear picture, won't they?'

He was startled by the glow which lit up her eyes. She showed him the corner where 'the man' waited and watched, and from that moment talked with great vitality, telling him again all she had told him and Felicity. This had started seven months ago. The man was always young; sometimes she thought it was invariably the same man. It did not matter where she went, she was followed, although she knew of no reason for it. She had a little money of her own, inherited last year from an uncle in Spain—she was quarter Spanish—and she supplemented her income by taking in knitting. She showed him her machine, with an unfinished blue cardigan on it. Obviously she was very proud of her good-quality work, and of the orders she obtained from large London stores.

'I'm not exactly a pauper, but no one would benefit from driving me out of my mind,' she said. 'Mr Dawlish, you will tell your friends that they *must* find out the truth, won't you?'

'Yes,' promised Dawlish; and before long he got up to leave her. When he was in the street, he saw her at the window. She did not wave, and looked scared again, as if by his leaving he had released all her fears.

Tim Jeremy was round the corner—near the spot where the man was supposed to stand and watch Marion Ard.

'Haven't noticed a soul take the slightest notice of you,' Tim announced. 'If you ask me, she dreams and visualises visions. All right, all right,' he added hastily, 'I know you want me to watch her for a day or two, Felicity told me. I'll fix it. You go and enjoy yourself like a rich industrialist instead of a man who keeps pigs.'

'Thanks, Tim,' said Dawlish. 'Try to keep the watch up for three days, then leave it for a day, and watch again on the fifth, will you? If you don't see anyone then, we can forget all about it.'

He caught the next train back to Haslemere, and reached home by half past eight, ravenous, delighted to find all the packing done, the labels written out and most of them stuck on the trunks and cases.

'I had such an excess of zeal I actually labelled both cabin trunks, and we're only taking one,' Felicity told him. 'We've plenty of labels, though, it doesn't matter. Did Tim say he would call us later tonight?'

'If he sees any mysterious men, he will. If we don't hear, we can forget it,' Dawlish told her. 'I asked him to let Ted talk to her, if he's back in time. Ted might be able to persuade her to take psychiatric treatment. Might help.'

'You really feel that she imagines it all, don't you?' asked Felicity.

'I think so,' agreed Dawlish. He stuck down the corner of a brightly coloured label on a trunk, then picked the trunk up. 'I'll take this one to the storeroom again,' he said. 'Amazing how light these things are when they're empty. If Tim rings up,' he added, 'I'll be the most surprised man in the south of England.'

He was not surprised.

2

LETTERS FROM HOME

'Darling,' said Felicity as she came into the cabin, 'there's a letter from Tim.'

'Didn't know he'd learned to write,' remarked Dawlish, from the hidden depths of the bathroom. 'What's it like out?'

'Hot.'

'Hot!'

'Not so bad as it was when we crossed the Equator,' said Felicity, standing in front of the dressing-table and mirror poking at odd pieces of hair, 'but nevertheless, hot, darling. About eighty-five in the shade, I'd say.'

'Oh, lor!' Dawlish emerged, dabbing himself with a large towel. It was when one saw him in the flesh, unexpectedly, that his vast size became really apparent; and so did the rippling power of his muscles. The two weeks' voyage to Cape Town had tanned him to an almost mahogany brown, and the only part of his body not so tanned was a small circular patch around the middle. 'Any other letters?'

'One from Joan, one from Old Josh. I'll bet he forgot whether to feed the pigs with the windfalls or the windfalls with the pigs.'

Felicity spoke very lightly, and without giving what she said any serious thought, for she was marvelling at this man she had married. He strode towards her and took Tim's letter, the only one for him; Tim had stuck blue *airmail* stickers over the envelope in so many places that it looked like a stamp collection in its own right. 'Darling,' Felicity went on, and now she was really paying attention, 'I don't see how it was possible without being positively shocking.'

'How what was possible?'

'Your sun tan. You couldn't have pulled your trunks down as far as *that*.' She pretended to be scandalised.

'That square yard on the top deck, reserved for the crew only,' Dawlish said absently, as he began to open Tim's letter. 'Only the crew saw me.'

'There are girls—'

'Now, you be a good sweet thing and read your letters,' said Dawlish, putting his right arm round her shoulders and giving her a hug which brought a gasp. Then he wound the towel round his middle and tucked it in, so that it looked as if he were wearing a sarong. That done, he opened the letter properly, and drew out the folded notepaper.

Felicity was not looking at her own mail.

'Curious?' asked Dawlish, straight-faced.

'Not half as curious as you. If you weren't burning to know what happened about Marion Ard you wouldn't have opened the letter until we'd reached Mozambique,' Felicity said. 'What does he say?'

Dawlish read, and announced, 'He hopes we're having a nice time.'

'Don't be a fool.'

'He hopes we don't have any ship-board romances.'

'Will you read that letter properly, or shall I take it?'

Dawlish skimmed the lines, and began to grin.

'She wasn't followed,' Felicity concluded.

'Dunno yet,' said Dawlish. 'The old devil has spun this nonsense out so that the meat of it's on the other side. From that, I'd say he's got a surprise for us.' He turned over, and although his smile did not go completely, it changed; and there was a glint in his eyes. 'Fel,' he said, 'she *was* followed.'

'*What?*'

'Fact. He says that the same man, a smallish man with dark hair and a bald patch, and down-at-heels shoes, followed her about London on two successive days.'

'I can't believe it.'

'I don't want to believe it,' Dawlish said, while the fan fluttered the notepaper in his hand, and he read on. 'Tim tried to follow this chap away from Marion's flat, but lost him.'

Felicity did not speak.

Dawlish read on very quickly, his eyes darting to and fro; gradually his smile faded completely, and bleakness replaced it. He had seldom looked more grim or more uncompromising than he did then. And, because of that, Felicity held her patience.

Dawlish looked up.

'She's disappeared,' he announced.

Felicity exclaimed: 'Oh, it *can't* be true.'

'Tim might joke, but not about this,' said Dawlish, and handed her the letter, then stood back and watched as she read. The warmth in the cabin had dried him already, although his hair was still damp. He went to his bed, dropped the towel and began to dress; when Felicity looked up, he was wearing lightweight slacks and his pink T-shirt vest, and squatting on a chair, putting on some open shoes.

'What do you make of it?' he asked.

'I can't make anything of it,' admitted Felicity, uneasily. 'Tim tried to follow this man twice, and lost him each time, and the third day Marion didn't leave her flat. He went to find out if she was all right . . ." *but couldn't get any answer, old boy. I didn't want to make too much fuss, so instead of calling the cops, I picked the lock. Flat was empty. I soon skedaddled, and I don't mind admitting I was up a tree.*" Felicity read all this out in a completely level voice, the context rather than the phrasing affecting her. "*I waited until the evening, and she didn't come back. Then I chivvied old pal Trivett, and he had one of the Yard chaps call at the flat. The landlady divvied up a key. The flat was still empty . . . and, to cut a long story in the middle, it still is. Marion A's disappeared, and so has Bald Spot. Trivett says that she's not officially missing until she's gone eight days, or some such nonsense, but he's promised to keep on the ball, and so has yours truly. P.S. Hope you're in the pink, as this finds me . . .*" Oh, the fool!' exclaimed Felicity, and put the letter down. 'It's unbelievable.'

'Not quite,' said Dawlish, soberly. 'She did say she was being followed, and we didn't believe her.'

'You did the next best thing.'

'Yes,' conceded Dawlish, and finished tying his shoes. 'Pity, its taken the edge off things, but we'll get over it. When was that posted?' He read the postmark. 'Saturday, so it took four days to get here. There might be another letter before we leave for Durban. If there isn't I'll telephone Tim.'

'She's probably turned up by now,' Felicity said.

They went out, pensive and quiet, to stand on deck for a moment and to look at the tablecloth of cloud which hung over Table Mountain. Except for that, the air was breathtakingly clear, showing how Cape Town nestled at the foot of the mountains, tiny and insignificant against their might. A smaller liner near by was moving off, and a crowd of a hundred or more Indians and Malays were watching it, the women in saris of such variety and beauty of colour that for a moment Felicity's thoughts were drawn from the missing girl. Flowers floated on the water, wishing the voyagers godspeed, and the beautifully dressed women were waving, while their men, mostly in white, stood quietly by.

'No, Pat,' Tim Jeremy said, his voice loud and clear one moment, the next rather faint. 'The girl hasn't turned up. She's now officially missing, and the police are looking for her all over the country. I'll cable if there's any news.'

'*No news,*' the cable waiting at Durban read. '*Love, Tim,*' Dawlish read as he stood on deck and looked at the Indian Ocean rolling against the bright yellow sands, and as he saw the tall, modern buildings which fringed the ocean, like a miniature Miami Beach. They could see the Buff; they could see the streets where the ricksha boys were doubtless dancing and prancing in their bright finery, broad black faces beaming; and they could see the side streets where, by night, the Zulu boys would strum their banjos and the Zulu girls would hum and dream, and there some boys and girls would sit on the kerb and nod and nod to sleep.

Dear Both (wrote Tim), *this has now become a* cause célèbre *and excuse anything wrong in the accents. The great British Press has decided that the Great British Public should know about the mysterious disappearance of Marion Ard, and I think the chief reason is the dearth of news. Nothing doing at all here, it doesn't even rain. Things should liven up next week, with Wimbledon and Henley and the next Test, but you never can tell. Marion A has now become a beautiful young heiress, because it transpires that she stood to inherit about fifteen thousand from an aged Spanish uncle. I've just seen her sister, a non-vindictive type, who says she never believed in this strange man. Have also talked to a lively up-and-coming lawyer, known as Os, to look after the legal side, so to speak. Thought it wise. Why don't you come home and solve it all in five minutes?*

Felicity read the letter for the third time as they strolled in the equatorial about the old fort at Mozambique. The fort, with its twenty-feet-thick walls, its old cannon, the balls massed in places like snooker blacks in small pyramids, was painted a white; so it reflected the fierce sun, and was almost hurtfully dazzling. From these walls, the tiny church, seeming to stand up in the sea as a lighthouse, was shimmering with wavy heat mirage. About them, prisoners sat stupidly in the heat, only one or two approaching near the Dawlishs or the other tourists to offer raffia hats, beautiful little hardwood carvings or flimsy paper knives. A wild-looking individual behind a massive door had hoisted himself up to a criss-cross of thick iron bars, and hung grimacing and gesticulating at them. A few khaki-clad soldiers, their muskets standing against the wall, gave a wide, white-toothed grin at everyone who passed.

'You wouldn't rather fly back, would you?' Felicity asked. She was tall and cool in a lemon-coloured sleeveless dress. Dawlish wore blue slacks and a short-sleeved shirt; his tan was more teak than mahogany.

'Not from here,' he said, 'but it's getting under our skins, Fel. At least you look fit enough to face anything!'

'I am, but what an odd thing to say,' said Felicity. 'What do you mean?'

Dawlish shrugged and grinned.

'Forget it,' he said. 'The words just came out without thinking.'

'Hi, there,' greeted a small, ebullient young man who had been the life and soul of the party without getting on anyone's nerves. 'How about a swim before we go back on board? There's the original swimming pool here, with dusky Portuguese East African beauties watching us from a distance.'

Two ricksha boys, old, grey-haired and listless in the shade, were watching with patient hope.

'We can swim on board. I'd much rather go round the town in one of these,' said Felicity, and immediately the boys sprang to life.

'Tommy, you take my wife,' Dawlish said to the ebullient passenger. 'I'll follow in the other chap, I'm quite enough weight for one.'

'Generous chap, your husband,' praised Tommy, beaming, and he helped Felicity in. 'This one's hood is a bit tattered, sure you wouldn't care for a better one?'

'This will do fine,' said Felicity.

Dawlish watched her, now so active and so fit; whatever else the cruise had done, it had been exactly what Felicity had needed. She was herself again, the operation and the long convalescence completely forgotten. She could even turn down a swim in favour of this drive in the blazing afternoon sun, past the tiny shops, each with a small doorway which looked like the entrance to a vast cave, watched impassively by groups of Africans.

He need no longer worry about Felicity, Dawlish knew.

There was no real need to worry about Marion Ard, but he had, from the moment of reading Tim's letter at Cape Town. He owed the girl nothing, and had done more than most people would to help; yet the fact that she was missing nagged at him. He could picture her huge eyes; her fears; her expression when his scepticism had shown so clearly on his face.

He suspected that Felicity thought a great deal about her, too, otherwise she would not have suggested that he might like to fly back home.

That was ridiculous; but it told him that Felicity knew full well that he could not get the thought of Marion Ard out of his mind. He was tempted to telephone Tim again, but that seemed absurd, too. If the girl was found, Tim would send a radio-telegram; if she wasn't, there was no point in harrassing himself.

When they went aboard, half an hour before dinner, Dawlish found himself looking at the cabin dressing-table, half expecting to see a cable. There was none. Dawlish stripped, had a welcome shower, and dressed with great care, so that he should not be wet with perspiration again; and he only half succeeded. Then Felicity came hurrying, quite gay, as if she had forgotten Marion Ard.

There was nothing for Dawlish at the next port of call: Mombasa.

There was nothing at Aden.

When they reached Alexandria, the shipping company's agent brought the mail on board, and Dawlish found himself waiting, almost on tenterhooks, unamused by the Arab salesmen who had surged aboard with carpets and carvings, fountain-pens and cigarette-lighters, 'ver cheap' snakes in baskets ready to be piped into action, postcards and guide-books, everything under the hot sun. Felicity was involved with a little party of women admiring some lace work; before long Felicity would buy.

A junior purser approached Dawlish, with a letter in his hand, and Dawlish almost pounced.

'A cable, sir,' the lad said. 'It's just arrived.'

Dawlish found a beaming smile for him, aware that in this young man, as in so many of the junior officers, there was a kind of hero worship for the deeds he was supposed to have done.

'Thanks very much,' he said. 'Do you always get mobbed like this on board?'

'Wait until this evening, sir, you won't be able to move on deck! You've made sure your cabin's locked, haven't you?'

'Firmly,' said Dawlish, and as the lad turned to go, he opened the cable.

It read starkly:

'*Body found. Strongly advise you fly home. Tim.*'

3

MORE NEWS

'Body,' said Felicity, and dropped on to the foot of the bed.

Dawlish had not shown her the cable until they were in the cabin, where even the blower blowing at its fiercest and the fan revolving at its swiftest could not cool the stifling heat.

'Oh, Pat, it's horrible.' When he didn't answer, Felicity went on: 'You had a kind of premonition, didn't you?'

'I don't believe in premonitions,' Dawlish replied, and tried to be casual. 'Since we first heard from Tim, it was obvious that the girl was in real trouble.'

'Why should Tim think you ought to fly home?' asked Felicity, with rebellion in her voice.

'That's the question,' Dawlish agreed. In a queer way, he did not really want to find the answer; there was something in that curt cablegram which conveyed a sense of acute alarm. 'He wouldn't suggest it unless he was really serious.'

'Will you telephone him?'

'We can't get ashore for a couple of hours, and the ship's telephones will be busy as soon as they're connected with the shore,' Dawlish said. 'Anyhow, if Tim had wanted to talk about this, he would have telephoned as soon as he knew we'd berthed—I'd get an incoming call at once.'

Felicity pushed a strand of damp hair back from her forehead. The cable and the heat together made her look flushed and unhappy.

'I suppose we'd better fly,' she said at last.

'There's no need for you to, sweet, no reason why we should both miss the Sphinx and the Pyramids.'

'Don't be ridiculous, of course I'm coming,' Felicity said, sharply. 'Oh, I'm so hot, I must have a shower.'

'I'm sorry, Mr Dawlish,' the airways official said, 'but there isn't a hope of getting two seats on a plane going home this week. I could fit you in on Monday.'

'How about one seat?' asked Dawlish.

'I could find one seat for tomorrow morning,' the official answered, 'but I would have to know at once whether you would take it, Mr Dawlish. It's one of those rush periods. I'm sorry I can't be more hopeful.'

'You're very good,' said Dawlish mechanically. 'I'll take the seat.'

Felicity would probably disbelieve him when he said that he tried to get seats for them both, but she knew so many of the other passengers that she would undoubtedly enjoy the trip to the ancient monuments of Egypt more than she anticipated.

He could not think much beyond the radiogram. Why should Tim summon him home; and why had he cabled instead of telephoned? He knew Tim too well to be in any serious doubt: Tim had not wanted to talk about it where they might be overheard, either at his end or on board. And Tim would not make a fuss about nothing.

'*Body found.*'

That poor kid.

* * *

There was nothing about the finding of the body in any of the English newspapers which had been flown to Egypt, and no news over the radio.

Felicity had been more understanding than Dawlish had expected, and was already on her way with a party of eight, in two huge American cars, towards the desert and the Pyramids and the ever-watchful Sphinx, towards a sunset of indescribable splendour which made beauty even out of the masses of tumbledown mud huts. Most of the passengers were ashore, as were many of the crew, and Dawlish had a solitary meal. He had an hour to spare when he finished, and decided to go to the main lounge for coffee. He was halfway up the big staircase when a youthful-looking man with a bald head and pince-nez glasses spun round a turn in the stairs, almost bumped into him, and then grabbed his arm, as if to steady himself.

Dawlish expected a gusty 'sorry!'

'Say,' said the bald-headed man, whose glasses were fitted with thick lenses, and who looked almost like a goggle-eyed baby in a pale grey linen suit. 'You Mr Dawlish?'

'Good evening,' said Dawlish, and tried not to speak woodenly.

'Just the man I was after,' said the other, and smiled quickly; he did everything quickly, even blinking. 'I'm Nimmo, of the *Daily Globe*. Can you spare me five minutes?'

Dawlish's defences were up on the instant.

'Have a heart,' he pleaded. 'I'm here on holiday.'

'What I want to know is, are you cutting it short to go home?' Nimmo's eyelids seemed to flash up and down, as if he were telegraphing a story back to London.

'Why should I?' Dawlish asked blankly.

'Playing the innocent, eh?' asked Nimmo, and looked as if he would like to poke Dawlish in the ribs. Then he moved down a step, so that they stood on the same tread; it was astonishing that he was more than a head shorter than Dawlish, a small, thin, unreal little man. 'Well, I can't say I blame you, but don't tell me that you don't know.'

'I haven't the faintest idea what you're talking about.'

Nimmo put a hand on Dawlish's arm, looked around as if with exaggerated fear of being overheard, put his lips close to Dawlish's ear and said:

'About the body in your trunk.'

They were only words, and at first they made no impact on Dawlish. 'About the body in your trunk.' The impact might have come sooner had Nimmo not been so exasperating with his conspiratorial manner, and the clutch of his hand. But Nimmo did nothing else to spoil the effect, except to move so that he could study Dawlish more closely.

He was not rewarded; no poker player could have kept a more impassive face. But the significance of what Nimmo had said struck Dawlish at last, and seemed to explode inside him. *About the body in your trunk.* And *Body found*, Tim had radiographed. *Strongly advise you fly home.* Add those together, and there was only one result: Tim and Nimmo must have been talking about the same body.

'Feeling a bit shaken, old chap?' asked Nimmo. 'Can't say I blame you, but I hand it to you for keeping a dead pan. Mind if I show what a clever little fellow I am? I was told that your wife's gone on to Cairo *via* the tombs of the Pharaohs, and you've booked a seat on the night's London plane. Still pretend that you didn't know about this?'

'I didn't know about this,' said Dawlish. There were times when it paid to be aloof with the Press, times when it would be absurd; now, it would have been absurd. 'Come and have a drink,' he added. 'I've half an hour to spare.'

'Ah, thanks.'

The lounge was huge, high-ceilinged and luxurious. A trio was on the dais, pianist, cellist and violinist, playing a supposedly lilting piece which sounded as if their instruments were drooping from the heat. Nimmo, bright and baby-faced, plumped for a long whisky and soda with a lot of ice; Dawlish abstemiously ordered black coffee.

'Off the record,' he said, 'a friend of mine cabled me to come home, and told me that the body of a girl I once tried to help had been found. That's everything I know. I'll be grateful if you can tell me more.'

'Not often I'm the bringer of really fresh tidings,' said Nimmo, but he was no longer so spritely, and in turn sounded cautious. 'I don't know a lot Dawlish, only that I had a cable from London a couple of hours ago. Here's the transcript.' He took a folded piece of paper out of his pocket and handed it to Dawlish, who maintained his impassive expression as he read:

Body of a young woman named Marion Ard found in trunk in home of Patrick Dawlish MI5, etc. etc. Body high after six weeks. Dawlish reported aboard Milton Castle, *due Alexandria tonight. Contact.*

Dawlish handed the transcript back.

'Thanks,' he said, and suddenly grinned broadly: 'Well, that's one out of the bag! Hell of a thing to happen, and you can tell the world that I resent my home being used for the storage of things like that.'

He had struck a wrong note.

He sensed the effect of that on Nimmo, and realised that he had tried too hard to be hearty. The trouble was in his past and his reputation: as a man who took nothing seriously, on the surface. But this was different, and he would have to be very careful how he acted.

'Naturally,' Nimmo said. Behind those thick lenses it was difficult to judge the expression in his eyes. He was suddenly self-deprecating. 'You know how it is, Mr Dawlish. I've my job to do, and with a man with a reputation like yours, my news-editor expects results. Any reason at all to think this is associated with espionage?'

'None at all,' said Dawlish. 'I haven't done a job for the secret service for seven years.'

Nimmo's eyebrows shot up.

'Really? You've worked with Scotland Yard a great deal, though, and are a personal friend of Superintendent Trivett, aren't you?'

'Yes.'

'Is it true you were once offered the post of Assistant Commissioner for Crime?'

'No comment.'

'So it was,' said Nimmo. 'Did you consult the police, or were you consulted by the police, about this Marion Ard, before you tried to help her?'

'No.'

'How did you try to help her? What was her trouble?'

Dawlish said very slowly: 'She thought that she was being followed by a man, and watched by a man, wherever she went. She asked me for help just before I left on the trip. I went to see her after she visited me, and arranged for a friend to keep an eye on her, although I thought she was dreaming this up. My friend told me that a man did actually follow her, and that she had disappeared two days after I'd left Southampton.'

Nimmo nodded, and asked:

'How often had Miss Ard been to see you?'

'She came once, and once only.'

'Thank you,' said Nimmo, and seemed to thaw again; perhaps he was getting more answers than he had expected. 'Why did you come on this cruise, Mr Dawlish?'

'My wife needed a long convalescence after a serious operation.'

'Did it affect your normal plans?'

'I keep a few pigs and grow a few apples and pears,' said Dawlish, 'and I've an old gardener and a boy who can handle things as well when I'm away as when I'm home. And now I ought to be on my way,' he added, and put his hands on the arms of his chair; in a single movement, he seemed to be towering over Nimmo.

'My car's alongside,' Nimmo said. 'Let me give you a lift.' They went down to Dawlish's cabin, where Dawlish collected an overnight case, and then went ashore, past swimming Arab boys waiting to dive for money, and a cacophony of Arab salesmen. Soon they were heading for the airfield along a wide road, behind an Arab driver gesticulating wildly with both hands, and ignoring the headlights of Nimmo's car.

They reached the airfield.

'Just one more question,' Nimmo said, as he slowed down at the entrance. 'How do you think the body reached your house, Mr Dawlish?'

'Someone put it there.'

'Who would do a thing like that?'

'That's what I want to find out,' Dawlish said, 'if the police haven't discovered it already.'

Nimmo didn't comment, but stopped outside the main entrance to the airport buildings. Dawlish got out, thanked him for the lift and was conscious of his questioning gaze. He had a feeling, the kind that Felicity would call a premonition, that Nimmo knew more than he had said.

The reporter drove off.

Dawlish heard aeroplane engines beginning to warm up; he should be home within twelve hours.

4

HOME

Two things were soon obvious when Dawlish reached London Airport. Tim was not here to meet him; but the police were. He recognised Detective-Sergeant Penfold of New Scotland Yard, a large and deceptively boyish-looking man, with a bright smile, reddish complexion and clothes which always looked a little too small for his massive body; but large though Penfold was, Dawlish outmatched him in size. With Penfold was a shorter, smaller man whom Dawlish did not remember seeing before. They were waiting in the approach to the customs bay, talking and smoking, and there was just a chance that they were not here for Dawlish.

Dawlish felt sure that they were.

He looked right and left, for Tim or anyone else he knew, but saw no one. This was the only customs bay being used at the moment. He was cleared with little fuss, picked up the one case and walked towards the exit doors, where he could get a taxi. It was a little after nine o'clock in the morning, and the sun outside looked as bright as Egypt's, although it was blessedly cool; almost too cool for his tropical suit.

Penfold and the other man came towards him.

Dawlish did not pretend to look surprised.

'Hallo, Sergeant, haven't seen you for a long time.'

'Must be six months, sir, mustn't it?' remarked Penfold; and Dawlish reminded himself how deceptive his quiet voice and friendly manner could be. 'Mrs Dawlish not with you?'

'She's seeing the Pyramids and things.'

'Very impressive, those Pyramids,' observed Penfold. 'I was out there during the war, you know; don't mind admitting I got tired of them, and fed up with eating sand. Going anywhere in a hurry, sir?'

'Home, as soon as I can. I suppose you know that Tim Jeremy sent for me.'

'I did understand that, yes.' Penfold was leading the way out, but the other man went ahead. As he passed, he looked at Dawlish much as a fly would look at a spider outside its web: with a mingling of respect and mistrust. He reached a car which was parked where no cars should be: in the taxi stand. The word 'police' was not visible on it, but this was as obviously a police car as Penfold was obviously a plain-clothes policeman.

'And a newspaperman in Cairo told me what it was all about,' Dawlish said, flatly.

'I assumed that you knew, sir,' Penfold commented. 'As you're so much nearer London than Haslemere, I wonder if you'd mind coming and having a little talk at the Yard?'

'Of course not. Is Superintendent Trivett in charge of the investigation?'

They reached the car. Penfold did not answer, but made a show of opening the door so that Dawlish could get in first. Dawlish bent almost double as he did so. Penfold climbed in after him, and there was a curious kind of finality about the way the door was slammed.

The smaller man took the wheel.

Penfold still hadn't answered; and Dawlish knew that he did absolutely nothing without a reason; everyone acquainted with him believed that he would go a long way at the Yard. His presence, his manner, even the present pause, had a disturbing cumulative effect. The affair of Marion Ard had begun to pluck at Dawlish's nerves from the moment Tim had said that he had seen a man following her; now the effect was sharper. He was more than uneasy; in different circumstances, he might have said that he was scared, but that was absurd.

They began the long drive out of the airport.

'As a matter of fact, sir,' Penfold said at last, 'Mr Trivett isn't in charge of this investigation, and he asked me to give you a personal message.'

Trivett was an old friend, a trusty, a man who had worked with Dawlish on investigations into many strange crimes. And here was Trivett, passing on a 'personal' message through a junior officer of the Yard. It was all of a piece; all added to that accumulation of anxiety which was leading fast to tension.

'What's the message?' asked Dawlish.

'He asked me to say that he was very sorry he wouldn't be available to take any part in this case, sir, as he's been assigned to an inquiry in France which is likely to take a long time. You know that he speaks French fluently, don't you? Always envied anyone with real control of a foreign language, I never had it myself. Remarkable how personnel changes even at the Yard, isn't it?' Penfold remarked glibly. 'Most of Mr Trivett's age group, if I can put it that way, have spread about, either to the Divisions or to the Provinces. Wouldn't be surprised if Mr Trivett found himself a nice little job as a chief constable in one of the counties, only needs a little bit of luck and a clear record!' Penfold was staring at the red traffic light which held them up at the exit. 'Cigarette, sir?'

'Thanks,' said Dawlish.

He was too subdued, and knew it; but he could not shake himself out of this unusual mood. It was as if there was a deliberate conspiracy to alarm him. Penfold had talked a lot to say a little: but the little was enough. Trivett had been given an assignment out of the country so that he could not work with him, Dawlish; and Dawlish's other friends in the Force had been posted to the Divisions. Penfold was telling him, with great care, that it was no use relying on his old association with Scotland Yard, that he had no special friend at court.

So Penfold was implying that he would need one.

'Feeling all right, sir?' Penfold asked, brightly.

'Good lord, no,' Dawlish flashed his smile, and had at least the satisfaction of startling the Yard man. This time he did not strike a false note, something like this had been needed. 'Would you feel all right if you'd discovered that someone had dumped the body of a girl in your house while you were away? I hate the idea. So will my wife.'

'Very unpleasant, sir.'

'Unpleasant's one word. I'd like to get the inquiries finished before my wife comes home, and she'll be about a week,' Dawlish said, more briskly still. 'Do you know how long the girl's body was in that trunk?'

'As far as we can tell, six weeks or so.'

God.

'How was it found?'

'Your gardener went into the house, to see that everything was in order,' Penfold explained, 'and he said he thought he smelt a dead rat. He suffers from sinus infection, and has a very poor sense of smell, or I'm sure he would have noticed something before. He found the body, and sent for the local police, and they took over. One man fainted,' Penfold added, and a pair of piercing blue eyes were suddenly turned to Dawlish; the look in them was almost accusing.

Dawlish said: 'So she must have been put there just after I left.'

'About that time, sir, we can't tell to a few days.'

He didn't actually say it, but he meant, 'Just after or just *before* you left.'

This situation was uglier than anything Dawlish had ever known one, and it fully explained Tim's caution. It probably explained the fact that Tim hadn't been at the airport; the police might have asked him to keep away.

'When was the body found?'

'Three days ago, sir, in the afternoon.'

There was a lot of traffic on the road. A giant aircraft was flying steadily overhead, the sun glistening on its windows and wings and fuselage. A heavy sand lorry, dripping water, was keeping up a steady forty miles an hour, and there was no chance to get past it.

'How did you identify the body?'

'A sister of the deceased identified certain pieces of jewellery, and the deceased's dentist identified some bridge work,' Penfold explained.

Dawlish had a vivid picture of Marion Ard snatching off her jewellery, of such pathetically little value, and thrusting it towards him as proffered payment for the 'help' she wanted. And he had not been convinced that she was really in danger.

'The sister, a Miss Ruby Ard, also told us that her sister had said she was going to see you,' Penfold went on, and it seemed as if he was drawing a cord a little tighter round Dawlish all the time. 'That was the last time the surviving sister saw her.'

'When was it?' asked Dawlish.

'May the 31st,' Penfold answered, and before Dawlish could

show any reaction, he went on: 'The day before you sailed, of course. That's the last time that Miss Ard was seen alive.'

'No it wasn't,' Dawlish said, quite sharply. 'Mr Jeremy saw her alive for the next two days.'

Penfold said, very mildly: 'Did he, sir?'

Dawlish almost snapped: 'You know damned well he did.' Instead he looked into Penfold's eyes, and smiled again, but not broadly; he was telling Penfold that he knew quite well what this was all about, and that it didn't rile him. But it scared him. That mild: 'Did he, sir?' carried a load of implication: that Tim had lied, that Tim hadn't seen the girl *or the man*, but had simply said so, because that was the best way to help his friend, Dawlish.

'Sergeant,' Dawlish said, as mildly, 'why don't you say exactly what you think?'

'Detective-Inspector, sir,' corrected Penfold. 'I've been promoted.' He smiled a cosy smile. 'This is my first solo investigation, so I'm anxious to get it over quickly. At this stage I don't think anything, but I know that you were one of the last persons, if not the very last, to see Miss Ard alive.'

5

COLDNESS

The sun was shining on the Thames, on the bright green of the plane trees on the Embankment, on the coloured awnings of the pleasure boats, on the massive might of the London County Hall, opposite New Scotland Yard. It shone upon the coat of arms embossed on the tall iron gates at the Yard, and on the police constables who stood on duty outside it, dressed in their thick serge, their heavy helmets, their massive boots. Dawlish knew this building, all of it, almost as well as he knew his own home. There had been the time, during the war, when he had actually had an office here, serving as liaison between the Yard and MI5. He had gone in and out for years, always exchanging a friendly word with the men on duty outside; even in the days when he had taken some absurd step which had antagonised the top men here, he had felt the sympathy and the liking of the lower ranks.

Working on his own, in the days soon after the war, when he had not been able to settle down, he had antagonised the top men even more; had exasperated even Trivett. But he had never known the time when a man would not return his wink.

No one he saw here looked as if they had ever seen him before.

Men whom he had known for years looked ahead as if they were deliberately ignoring him; and, of course, they were. He had known the Yard angry, hostile, even livid; but he had never known it indifferent to him.

'What exactly do you want from me?' he asked Penfold.

'I'd just like to ask you a few questions,' Penfold answered, 'and I'm sure you'll have no objection to answering.' He stopped at a waiting-room door, and smiled his slow, boyish smile. 'You won't mind waiting here for a few minutes, will you?'

Dawlish faced him, smiled back and said:

'Provided it isn't more than a few, Inspector.' He glanced at his watch; it was five past ten. 'I'll wait until twenty-minutes past ten, if you're not back by then, you'll have to excuse me.'

'I'll try not to be so long.'

Penfold hadn't liked that stipulation; and Dawlish had not meant him to. There was cold hostility under this cloak of civility and almost excessive courtesy, and it might help to rattle Penfold; if the man could be rattled. Certainly he must not be allowed to think that he could have everything his own way.

Penfold opened the door.

Inside were two rooms, each leading off a small square compartment; one room door was open, the other closed. The first room was empty, and Dawlish went in. There was a table, three upright chairs and a photograph, at least fifty years old, of a bewhiskered policeman; an Assistant Commissioner of whom Dawlish had never heard. The walls were distempered green, rather like a hospital ward. There was a small window, and at least that wasn't barred.

Many men and women had waited here until Yard detectives had come and first questioned and then arrested them; many

now dead of hanging. Many now serving long terms of impris-
onment had sat on these chairs and tapped ash into this same
green porcelain ash-tray. Dawlish lit a cigarette, and immediately tapped the ash; then realized that it was a nervous gesture,
there had been no need. Well, it wasn't surprising that he was
on edge; this crisis had been building up for weeks, although he
had never expected anything quite like this.

Where the devil was Tim?

The police knew that he and Tim had worked together for
nearly twenty years; that between them existed a friendship and
a loyalty which nothing could break. The police knew that Tim
would gladly, cheerfully and persistently lie if he thought that
Dawlish was in trouble. They had plenty of grounds for suspicion in general, but none in particular.

He finished the cigarette in six minutes, so had eight more
minutes to wait. If he smoked another cigarette, it would look
as if he was smoking to calm his nerves; so he didn't light one.
He began to wonder if Penfold would keep him waiting over the
fifteen minutes, so as to force a kind of climax. Dawlish began to
smile, but did not relax. There were so many things he wanted
to do: find out exactly what had happened, read all the newspapers, talk to Old Josh, talk to Tim, find out about this small man
with the dark hair and the bald patch. That man held the clue to
the truth of Marion Ard's murder, and must be found.

Were the police looking for him?

Or had they taken it for granted that he, Dawlish . . .

This wasn't making sense.

He kept looking at his watch and listening for footsteps.
With a minute to go, he felt sure that Penfold would not come.
With a quarter of a minute to go, he was standing tensely by
the door, hoping that at the last moment the man would arrive,
so that there would be no need for any gesture of defiance. The

minute hand ticked away with impersonal relentlessness; and the quarter of an hour was up.

Dawlish opened the room door; then the passage door. A uniformed policeman was on duty outside, and looked surprised to see Dawlish.

'Want something, sir?'

'No, thanks.' Dawlish smiled at him, and turned towards the corner of the passage. He wasn't really sure that this was wise, and resented the need for it; but if he had to have a clash with Penfold or anyone else at the Yard, it might as well begin now.

The constable said hastily: 'Excuse me, sir, but Mr Penfold will be back shortly.' He caught up with Dawlish, and put a restraining hand on his arm; not tightly, just enough to assert his authority. 'He won't be long, I'm sure.'

Dawlish freed himself, without trouble, and turned in the wide, bare passage to face the man, who was middle-aged and rather tired-looking.

'Officer, have you any authority to detain me?'

'Well, no, sir, but Mr Penfold said he'd be back, and—well, I'm just here to see if there's anything you want. Shall I send a message to Mr Penfold?'

'Give him one,' Dawlish said. 'Tell him that he'll find me at my home.' He smiled again, bleakly, and the man did not know what to do. Dawlish walked briskly towards the corner, wondering what would happen if he barged into Penfold. He told himself that the sensible thing would be to go back and talk to the man; a few minutes' delay was really unimportant. But the issue involved was vital.

No one was in sight along the next passage. At the end of it was the landing, the big, open grille lift, and the staircase. The lift was in motion; he could hear it humming and see the cables going up and down. He went down the stairs, without hurrying.

On the ground floor there were several uniformed policemen and two plain-clothes men, including the thin one who had been with Penfold. He was startled at sight of Dawlish.

'Good morning,' Dawlish said, and nodded curtly and started for the door.

'Excuse me, sir, have you just come from Mr Penfold?'

'No,' said Dawlish. 'Apparently he had more important things to do, and I've too much on my mind to sit waiting for him, here or anywhere else. I've told the constable that I'll be at my home.'

This was something beyond the plain-clothes men's experience; people who were asked to wait at the Yard always waited. A grey-haired sergeant at the desk was staring, and two constables were watching Dawlish. He reached the top of the steps, and no one tried to stop him, although it was obvious that all of them would like to.

So there was no warrant out for him.

Of course there wasn't; what the devil was the matter with him?

He went briskly down the steps. It might have been imagination, but everyone in sight seemed to pause to stare at him. He reached the foot, half expecting a shout or a whistle, or some sign to say that he was to be stopped, but none came. He went towards Parliament Street and Whitehall, not to the Embankment, and as he approached the iron gates and the guard on this side, he felt sure that he would be stopped.

He was not.

He felt sticky and hot when he stepped into Parliament Street, and he didn't see a taxi. He wanted one badly, needed to get rid of the feeling that everyone was watching him. He liked none of this at all, and was still not sure that he had done the right thing. He might have angered Penfold; and Penfold might have left him, deliberately, to find out whether it was bravado or not when he had set a time limit.

A taxi came along, empty. Dawlish waved to it, and the taxi slowed down. He climbed in, and looked along the narrow street towards the courtyard he had just left, and saw a police car coming out. He was not sure that it was Penfold's, but it looked much the same. The car turned left, as he said to the taxi-driver, 'Victoria, please.' The station wasn't far away; ten minutes, at most. Dawlish sat back, lit another cigarette, and every now and again looked through the window, to find out if the car from the Yard was still behind him.

It was.

It pulled up just behind the taxi at Victoria. He expected the two men in it to jump out and come hurrying after him, but only one got out, a tall, youthful-looking fellow with almost gingery hair. He did not speak to the driver, but strolled after Dawlish, who knew the times of the trains by heart; he had fifteen minutes to wait. He bought a first-class ticket, and the man from the Yard went to the booking office immediately after him; Dawlish heard him say, '. . . Haslemere.' Dawlish went to the central bookstall, bought all the morning newspapers and tucked these under his arm, then strolled towards the platform. The train was in, and almost empty. He selected an empty compartment, got in, and pretended not to notice the Yard man enter the compartment next door. He sat in a corner and began to read through the newspapers, seeking news about Marion Ard's murder.

All but the *Daily Globe* carried a paragraph or two, but nothing really sensational; this was old news, now. But it was disturbing to read:

Scotland Yard officers joined members of the Surrey C.I.D. at Four Ways, the home of Major Patrick Dawlish, where the body of Miss

Marion Ard was found in a trunk, after being missing for nearly six weeks.

Major Dawlish is still away, and it is understood that he is some- where in Africa.

Anyone who read that would jump to the conclusion that he had cut and run for it; a lot of people were likely to be surprised when he showed up at Haslemere, and then in Alum village.

He turned to the *Globe.*

The thick lenses of Nimmo's pince-nez seemed to shimmer from the pages. This was a front-page spread, and there was a photograph of Dawlish, as well as one of Marion Ard; a photo- graph taken when she had been a year or two younger. Dawlish thought she looked no more than seventeen or eighteen. There was much wistfulness about her, obvious even so long ago.

The *Globe* had it all: that he, Dawlish, was flying home to assist the police in their inquiries, that he had only seen the dead woman once, that she had told him that a man was following her everywhere, and that she had begged for his help. The undoubted fact was that all of it seemed unreal; just as the girl had seemed unreal. Few who read this would take the story seriously; this, it seemed to say between the lines, is Dawlish's cock-and-bull story; does he think our readers are a lot of gull- ible fools?

He read every word.

He wished he had the old newspapers, so that he could see what had been said before.

The train started off, and ten minutes out of the station, the restaurant-car man came along, calling, 'Coffee and light refreshments now available, please take your seats.' The man was an old-stager on this line, and Dawlish knew him well. He peered in, then actually backed away from the door.

43

'Hallo, George,' greeted Dawlish. 'Think you could bring me some coffee here? I don't feel like being on show.'

'Yes—yes, of course, Mr Dawlish. I—I thought you were away.'

'Had to come back to find what this bad business was about.'

'Yes, Mr Dawlish, of course. I won't keep you long for your coffee, sir.'

George hurried on, and forgot to announce coffee and light refreshments at the next few compartments. Dawlish lit another cigarette, and settled down. Half a dozen attendants from the refreshment car found an excuse to look at him. His coffee arrived, piping hot. He sat back and pretended to doze, but there was no thought of dozing in his mind. When the train approached Haslemere he got up and found the Yard man already in the corridor.

'Wasted journey,' Dawlish said. 'I'm still here.'

The man was human enough to grin. 'Well, we can't take chances with a man like you, sir, can we?'

They certainly weren't taking any chances.

The porters gaped, the ticket-collector forgot to say good morning, and people in the station yard stopped to look at Dawlish. The taxi-driver he approached glanced past him towards the Yard man, as if he thought he needed permission to accept Dawlish as a fare.

'Remember where I live?' asked Dawlish. 'Straight there, please.'

'Yes, sir, right away!' The man started the engine, and a local police car followed Dawlish, with the Yard man in it. Dawlish did not even need to glance out of the window to check; the way the driver kept looking into the mirror told its own tale. Dawlish had to force himself to lounge in the old cab, and to make it look as if he was unconcerned. In fact, his mind was in turmoil, because there was so little he understood. At least he would feel better when he had seen exactly what there was to see here, talked to Old Josh, and talked to Tim.

He looked nostalgically upon the familiar countryside, the grass longer and the foliage of the trees thicker than when he had left. There was a fork in the road, just beyond Alum village, and the taxi turned left, towards Four Ways. Then it came in sight, a mock-Tudor house some thirty years old, built solidly, and looking attractive at the top of the steep drive. Dawlish had known many kinds of home-coming, but nothing to match this.

Two policemen were standing outside the drive gates. Dawlish saw them move aside as the taxi drew nearer and was obviously going to turn into the drive. Then he forgot the policemen.

On the other side of the road was a kind of recess, made so that large cars could turn out of the drive without difficulty; in this recess a young woman was standing by the side of a pale blue motor-scooter.

That in itself was not particularly surprising.

The woman was: she was so like Marion Ard that she was almost certainly the dead girl's sister.

6

RUBY ARD

The girl obviously recognised Dawlish from photographs; he could tell that from the way her expression came to life, and the way she moved forward, with a hand outstretched. He thought she was going to touch the door of the taxi, but she did not. The driver slid into low gear, swung into the drive and rasped towards the house. Another police constable was on duty at the open front door, watching as if without interest. The taxi pulled up in front of him; he opened the door for Dawlish, respectfully, and touched his helmet. This was the first really friendly gesture from the police, but he had known this man for nearly fifteen years.

'Hallo, Pike; how are you?'

'Fit as ever, sir, thanks.'

'You might have stopped this happening while I was away,' said Dawlish, paying the driver off. 'Who's here?'

'Chief Inspector Smith, sir, and Detective-Sergeant Harrison, from Scotland Yard.'

Smith was new to Haslemere, having been moved from another part of the country; Dawlish knew of the man, but had never met him. Certainly they were making sure that he had no friends at court. He was beginning to feel deeply angered, but knew that he must not show it. He resented the way that the house and grounds had been taken over, but that was unreasonable resentment; one of the dangerous factors was that he was in a mood to be unreasonable.

He had hoped to see Tim.

'Mr Jeremy here?'

'No, sir. He was yesterday morning, but I haven't seen him since. He went up to London, I think, to see Mr Penfold.'

'Ah, yes.' Dawlish nodded.

The taxi was halfway down the drive and pulling over to one side, because the girl was coming up on her motor-scooter. What on earth had brought her, and why had she been waiting? Dawlish did not feel like an encounter with an emotional young woman, but could hardly refuse to see the girl, although there was no reason why he should go to meet her. He went indoors. Everything was so familiar that the moment brought another wave of nostalgia; the only thing missing was Felicity coming out of the drawing-room, or hurrying down the wide oak staircase towards the extensive domestic quarters, where men were talking. Here was the large, modern kitchen, the passage leading from it, and the storerooms and pantries. Dawlish wondered which room the body had been found in, then realised where it must have been, and in what trunk: the one which Felicity had labelled in error, and which he himself had carried to the storage-room.

A tall, sharp-featured man in a pale grey suit, more like a doctor or lawyer to look at than a policeman, was standing in the doorway of this room; this was Superintendent Smith. By his side was a tubby man whom Dawlish recognised as Harrison of the Yard's Finger-print Department, one of the up-and-coming young men, with curly brown hair, baggy brown suit and shiny brown shoes.

Smith nodded curtly.

'Good morning, Mr Dawlish.'

'Hallo, sir,' Harrison greeted breezily enough.

''Morning,' returned Dawlish, and felt resentment rising against Smith's coldness. He had to remind himself that Smith, Penfold and everyone associated with the police side of the case, accepted the possibility that he had killed the girl. They might even go further than that, and feel sure. Not quite sure what to say next, a cold wind seemed to blow about him as he stood there. The police knew him well, they had always been well disposed, they would only adopt this coldly hostile attitude if there were good reasons for believing that he was guilty.

What reasons could they have?

There was a ring at the front-door bell. He felt sure that it was the dead girl's sister, and found himself wondering why she had rung the bell instead of asking the policeman on duty to come and tell him; perhaps the policeman had refused to leave his post. The two detectives were studying him, still waiting for him to speak, but the only things to say were trite and this was no time for triteness.

The bell rang again.

He asked with more abruptness than he meant: 'Do you know who killed the girl yet?'

Smith said as curtly: 'No.'

Harrison put in: 'Have to be absolutely sure in a case like this.'

'Or any case,' Dawlish said, and added tartly: 'I hope.' He was losing his patience again; if they were setting out to antagonise him, they were certainly succeeding. He wanted time to think this out, and had none; certainly he wanted time before he talked to the dead girl's sister.

'Oh, be sure of that, sir,' Harrison soothed.

'Is there anything I can do to help?' Dawlish asked.

'I understand that you were not particularly anxious to be helpful at Scotland Yard,' Smith said.

'Ah,' said Dawlish, and found it easier to smile. 'I see what's under your skin. You'll find me ready, even eager, to co-operate, Inspector, if you apply the ordinary courtesies, and if you at least appear to accept the old axiom about men being innocent until they're found guilty.' He felt better; no one could take exception to any of this. 'No one has yet asked me whether I killed Miss Ard, but the implication is quite evident. The answer is that I did not. And judging from your attitude and that of Penfold at the Yard, it is extremely important that you should find out who did.' He smiled again. 'There is nothing I won't do to help.'

The bell rang again.

'Excuse me, won't you?' he said, and turned and walked away; he heard Harrison say something under his breath, but couldn't be sure what it was. He stepped into the kitchen, where the bell had rung, and looked up at the indicator; the red disc of the front door was swaying to and fro. Marion Ard's sister was almost certainly still there. He pushed his fingers through his wiry hair, and found that his forehead was damp. There was another factor, too: he had eaten very little on the aircraft, and was hungry.

He could not keep the girl waiting much longer.

He went into the passage through the empty house. It was her all right, standing just inside now, with the policeman close to the front door, as if to make sure that she didn't come right in. She was remarkably like her sister about the eyes and forehead, but had a fuller mouth and a rather larger chin; so she was nearer real beauty than the dead girl, but had none of that elfin or fey look; she was likely to be blunt and straightforward, standing no nonsense from anyone. She wore a pair of well-cut dark blue slacks, a jumper of lighter blue, and a zipper-type lumber jacket coat, all just right for the motor-scooter. She had a clean, fresh, windswept look about her as she waited for Dawlish to approach; and he had never been more aware of anyone's appraisal.

She was a head taller than her sister, and slimmer; a nice figure, although not big anywhere.

Dawlish did not have to recognise her, so he greeted:

'Good morning.'

She said, very slowly and deliberately: 'I'm Sister Ruby.'

Dawlish looked puzzled.

'I don't think we've met.'

'We haven't met,' Ruby Ard said, 'but you must know who I am; you've heard so much about me.'

Why should she say that?

Dawlish was aware of the policeman, standing as near as he reasonably could, obviously making sure that he should not miss a word; at the first chance he would rush to a superior with an account of this meeting. But the constable was only one consideration. Far more important was the steady gaze of this slim, rather attractive girl, and the complete assurance of the way she had said, '. . . you've heard so much about me'.

'I don't know why you should say that,' responded Dawlish, and stood aside. 'But I can see who you are, now.'

'We're very much alike, aren't we?' Ruby Ard didn't move.

'I didn't know your sister well,' said Dawlish, contrarily, 'but I shouldn't have said you were really alike, except at the eyes and forehead.' He motioned to the drawing-room, the door of which stood open. 'Won't you come in?'

Had she been a different type, he would have expected some kind of an emotional outburst; even hysterics. No one had ever looked less hysterical. She hesitated for a moment, then went into the drawing-room, where the curtains were drawn as Felicity had left them, to keep the sun off the carpet and the furniture. Dawlish pulled the centre curtains back. As far as he knew, no one except the police had been in here since he and Felicity had left, there was a film of dust everywhere. He saw traces of the police visitation, in smears of grey powder, and in items of furniture which had been shifted; that was all.

Ruby Ard looked swiftly yet appraisingly about the room, and then back into Dawlish's eyes.

'You have all this,' she said, 'and yet you had to do that to poor Marion.'

Dawlish's back was towards the window, and the daylight shone full on to her face. Where her sister's eyes had been limpid and appealing, hers were bright and starry; almost too hard. She had dark hair, most of it concealed by a bright scarf which was tied in pirate fashion, with the ends hanging down her back.

'I don't know what you think, Miss Ard,' Dawlish said flatly, 'but I did nothing to your sister except try to help her.'

Her eyes asked, 'And you expect me to believe that?'

'I want to find her murderer,' Dawlish went on, 'and I also want to find out why he chose to hide her body in my house.'

'As you were going away, wasn't it very convenient for you?' There was sharpness in her voice.

Something seemed to snap in Dawlish, and he spoke as sharply, and roughly.

'I didn't kill her, I didn't put her in the trunk, I didn't know she was here. If you've come to reproach a murderer, you're wasting your time. Your sister came here and told me that she was frightened, that she was followed and watched by a strange man. I tried to help her. I don't know what happened when I went away, but I left her at her flat in Kensington, alive and well if still frightened. That's the truth and that's where I'm working from. Do you want to find her murderer?'

Ruby Ard did not attempt to find an answer.

'Well, do you?' demanded Dawlish. 'Or have you jumped to conclusions, like the police, probably like the rest of the world? If you have, you're no use to me, and I've no time to spare. I've a lot to do.'

Unexpectedly, Ruby asked quietly:

'What use would I be if I had an open mind?'

'You could help to find the murderer. You could tell me more about Marion, her girl friends, her men friends, how long she had been living on her nerves, all the things that might help to find out why she was killed, and who killed her.'

Ruby began to smile, and so startled Dawlish again. The smile was not really one of amusement, but more of surprise. He saw how beautiful her eyes were when the expression in them was softer.

'You don't know very much, do you?' she said, in that still, quiet voice. 'Marion didn't know it, but she was to inherit fifteen thousand pounds from an uncle who bequeathed me a few books and heirlooms. But I was Marion's next of kin. As a result of her death, I inherit her fortune. So we've something in common: I'm under suspicion, too.'

Her lips twisted in that wry smile, and her eyes took on the blueness and the clearness of the summer sky.

Dawlish thought: 'It would be easy to trust and as easy to be fooled by her.'

'We could call that something in common,' he agreed.

'What I really want to find out is whether the man or men Marion talked about did exist, or whether she dreamed them up,' Ruby said, firmly. 'She lived in a world of her own, but you must know that. Did *you* see any man?'

Tim had, but wasn't here to say so.

'A man or men existed,' Dawlish answered. 'I am sure—'

Before he could go on, he heard the sharp hoot of a car horn, and turned and looked out of the window, hoping to see Tim. Instead, he saw Penfold, with the smaller Yard man sitting next to him; and if Penfold's expression was any guide, he meant business.

7

INTERROGATION

'Do you know who this is?' Ruby Ard asked, quickly.

'I know Detective-Inspector Penfold very well,' Dawlish said, 'and you sound as if you've met him before.'

'He always behaves as if he's sure I helped to kill Marion.'

'If it's any consolation, he uses the same approach to others,' said Dawlish dryly. He looked through the window into Penfold's challenging eyes and, quite unexpectedly, found himself clasping Ruby's hands; they were very cool. 'Would you like to stay?'

'He'll never allow it.'

'Won't he?' murmured Dawlish, and released her and went to the door. He knew exactly how to treat Penfold now; knew that the time had passed when he need be so obviously on the defensive. Penfold was getting out of the car, almost glaring into the hall; the policeman on duty was standing stiffly to attention.

Dawlish's smile might have been for his closest friend.

'Hallo, Inspector, nice to see you.' He stood by the open door, hand stretching out as Penfold came within reach; Penfold found his hand gripped. 'And most obliging of you to come out here to see me,' Dawlish went on. 'Do you mind if I start with a question?'

Penfold was a big, blond boy, wondering where the catch was. 'What question?'

'Do you know where Tim Jeremy is?'

'No, I don't,' answered Penfold. 'I've been trying to find him for twenty-four hours. Don't *you* know?'

It was one shock after another, but this need not be a development for the worse; it would be characteristic of Tim to hide from the police until he'd had a chance to talk to Dawlish. So far, there had been no opportunity to get in touch.

'I haven't the faintest idea,' Dawlish said, and led the way into the drawing-room. 'I believe you know Miss Ruby Ard.'

'We've met,' said Penfold. Dawlish had shaken him, and he was not at his best; he looked and probably felt gawkish. 'Mr Dawlish, I'd like to see you alone, please.'

The detective-sergeant was hovering in the doorway, a little vaguely; the fact that he looked so unimpressive probably meant that he was good at his job.

'Inspector,' said Dawlish, 'I've nothing to say to you or anyone else that Miss Ard and the whole wide world can't hear, and I'd rather not talk to you alone. I don't know what's in your mind, I do know that when I last saw Marion Ard she was alive, and that she must have been brought here after I left for the ship at Southampton. Can we start from there?'

'You know perfectly well that there may be questions prejudicial to yourself and Miss Ard,' Penfold said. 'What are you being so difficult about, Mr Dawlish? If you've nothing on your conscience, you've nothing to fear from being questioned. Isn't it time you co-operated with the police instead of giving cause for suspicion that you have something to hide?'

'If I go, neither of you will have to give way, will you?' asked

Ruby, and she moved towards the door with long, graceful strides. 'May I wait, Mr Dawlish?'

'Of course.'

'Would it be a sin if I had a look in the larder?'

'You won't find much there,' Dawlish told her, but his eyes kindled at the thought of food. 'Why don't you pop down to the village shop and get some bread, butter, ham say, and anything else you can think of? Tell them it's for the Dawlish account, they know the kind of thing we like, too. Oh, and some milk.'

'All right, I will,' Ruby said, and went out.

Dawlish found himself watching her long-legged figure, and the brightness of her clothes. He was aware of Penfold and the sergeant appraising him with that edge of suspicion which had been there all the time. He made himself turn away from the window, although, had he had his choice, he would have watched the girl ride down the drive.

'Close the door, King, please,' Penfold said.

The sergeant obeyed.

'Cigarette?' invited Dawlish, and held out his case.

'No, thank you. Mr Dawlish, I have to warn you that your sudden departure from New Scotland Yard this morning was highly prejudicial. I hope you won't think it necessary to do anything like that again.'

'I hope it won't be necessary to go to the Yard as a suspect again,' murmured Dawlish.

'No one has accused you of anything, Mr Dawlish.'

'That is precisely why I can stand by my rights,' Dawlish countered, and grinned. 'Do we have to fight all the time? You know my line, and I know yours. If I can help, I will. After all, I've a stronger reason than you for wanting to find the murderer. Were you serious about Tim Jeremy?'

'Mr Jeremy was asked to call at Scotland Yard to see me

yesterday morning and he did not arrive,' declared Penfold. 'Since then, all reasonable attempts to trace him have been made, but he is not at his home or his club, or with any of his friends or your mutual friends. May I advise you to tell him that he is serving no useful purpose by behaving like this?'

'Had you made it clear that you thought he was a liar, too?' asked Dawlish, mildly.

'Mr Jeremy stated that he had seen Miss Marion Ard after you had left England. I have found no one else—not her landlady, none of the shops where she calls for business, none of the tradespeople she dealt with—who have seen her since the evening of May 31st.'

'Where did Tim say he'd seen her?'

'That is irrelevant.'

'Wasn't it Tim who first reported that she was missing?'

'Yes, it was,' agreed Penfold, 'but her landlady was on the point of reporting it. Mr Jeremy must have realised that a report was inevitable before long, and so realised that there was no point in withholding the information any longer.'

'You don't like Tim a bit, do you?' Dawlish was tart.

'I have no reason to doubt Mr Jeremy's statement,' said Penfold, flatly, 'but I intend to check it very closely. Mr Dawlish, how long had you known Miss Marion Ard?'

'For about five hours.'

'When did you first see her?'

'On the afternoon of May 30th.'

'When did you last see her?'

'Early evening, on the same day.'

'You're not under oath, Mr Dawlish, but I hope that you will watch what you say.'

'If this were under oath, the answers would be precisely the same,' Dawlish said.

The danger was in the way Penfold got under his skin, riling him so badly. Of course, that was intended, and if he let his exasperation show itself, it would be a triumph for Penfold. He heard the distant *pop-pop-pop* of the motor-scooter on its way, but did not look out of the window.

'When did you first hear from Miss Ard?' demanded Penfold.

That was easy.

'About a week before she came here. I had a letter telling me she was in great danger, and asking me to help her. I advised her, by letter, to go to the police. She wrote again, and telephoned two or three times; and I gave her the same advice each time. Finally she came here.'

'Without an appointment?'

'Out of the blue.'

'Doesn't it strike you as peculiar, Mr Dawlish, that she should show such insistence with a man whom she did not know?'

'I have a kind of reputation,' Dawlish said dryly, 'and she had probably read about it.'

'Did she say why she preferred help from you, instead of the police?'

'That wouldn't be self-evident, would it?'

Penfold snapped: 'Where are those letters, Mr Dawlish?'

'The letters which Marion Ard wrote?'

'Yes.'

'In the bureau over there,' said Dawlish, pointing to a mahogany bureau in a corner, where Felicity did all her letter-writing, 'or in the desk in my room—I've a small study on the other side of the passage.'

'Didn't you take these letters away with you?'

'I've just told you where you'll find them.'

'Don't you think it a remarkable thing,' Penfold asked, in a silky voice, 'that in our search of this house, a very thorough search, we have found no letters from Marion Ard? None was in the bureau, none was in the desk. When a body is found in a house, as this poor girl's body was found here, we search very thoroughly, Mr Dawlish.'

This was triumph; and Penfold nearly gloated.

Dawlish checked himself from going to the bureau; it would be a waste of time, and would only enable Penfold to gloat in earnest. If the police hadn't found those letters, they weren't here. Yet he was quite sure that they had been; now that he was forced to concentrate, he was positive that they had been in the bureau, because he had read them in this room, with Felicity present, after getting back from London.

So whoever had brought the girl's body here had searched and stolen those letters.

'Well?' Penfold shrilled.

'Yes,' said Dawlish. 'I think it's most remarkable.'

'I am asking you, Mr Dawlish, whether those letters were ever written.'

Dawlish said: 'They were written and received.'

'Who saw them?'

'My wife and I.'

'Who else?'

'No one else.'

Dawlish was beginning to feel the icy breath of fear, and also to understand more clearly why Penfold had taken the line he had. He was realising something else, too: this was the kind of questioning that he might expect in the witness-box. He could even think it possible that he would find himself in one, giving evidence on his own behalf.

'Mr Dawlish,' Penfold went on, as if he were near the end of his patience, 'is it not true that you have for many years been a close personal friend of Superintendent Trivett, of the Criminal Investigation Department?'

'Yes.' As if Penfold didn't know.

'Has it not been your custom when individuals have applied to you for assistance, to pass them on to the police and, if they wouldn't take that advice, inform Mr Trivett of the situation?'

'I have done it that way, yes.'

'In this case, you say you were about to leave for a long cruise. The girl was a stranger. You felt sufficiently interested in her to go to London and see her. You asked your friend Jeremy to keep an eye on her—I am quoting him. You had no personal interest in this young woman whatsoever, you were on the eve of departure, with a lot to do, and yet you preferred to handle this situation personally, and did not even trouble to telephone Mr Trivett, although, if the young person was in fact in danger, the police were the obvious people to be advised.'

Dawlish kept a stony face.

'It isn't the first time I've tried to help where the police have refused.'

'Refused, Mr Dawlish?' Penfold drew a step nearer. 'Are you saying that she had applied for help, and was refused?'

'Yes.'

'Mr Dawlish,' said Penfold, with a great sigh, 'it may interest you to know that there is no trace of a visit by Marion Ard to New Scotland Yard or to any of the divisional police stations in London. The records have been closely checked.'

Dawlish made no comment; he was too badly shaken by a statement which he was bound to accept on its face value; certainly Penfold would not lie.

'*Well*, Mr Dawlish?'

'Marion Ard told me she had been to Scotland Yard,' Dawlish said, 'and I believed her.'

He remembered thinking of Ruby Ard: that it would be easy to trust her, and as easy to be fooled by her. He had trusted her sister up to a point, and it might prove to have been a deadly mistake. He had believed everything, except the story of the man who had frightened her, and had believed she was convinced of his existence. And one had existed. But if she had lied about going to the police, what else had she lied about?

And why had she lied?

He felt a pounding in his mind, as of the dawn of a new kind of comprehension. First the missing letters, now this evidence, were pointing to just one thing: it had been no coincidence that the body of the girl had been found here. It had been put here with consummate skill, too; the evidence had built itself up remorselessly.

There was another factor, one which had been visible in the distance before, but was much closer now. On the strength of all this, Penfold might think he had a strong enough case to make a charge. He would want to feel sure; but if all this circumstantial evidence had been considered by the legal experts at the Yard, and Penfold had been given authority to make an arrest, now would be the moment for it.

Dawlish had never felt more alone, seldom in greater danger.

8

QUEST FOR TIM

Penfold was studying Dawlish intently, and Detective-Sergeant King was standing by the door, as if he half expected the big man to make a dash for freedom. Dawlish waited woodenly, but his heart was pounding. In the distance he heard the *pop-pop-pop* of that motor-scooter returning, and he had to admit that Penfold had been right not to have Ruby Ard here during the interview.

Was Penfold about to recite the formula of arrest?

'Mr Dawlish,' said Penfold, very deliberately, 'in the course of the next few days while inquiries are going on, it may be necessary to interview you from time to time, perhaps at short notice. I must ask you to remain in this vicinity, and to inform the local police if at any time you intend to go to London or elsewhere.'

So it was a reprieve; they were not certain, yet.

'Fair enough,' Dawlish said, and tried to conceal the extent of his relief.

'There is another matter,' went on Penfold, and Dawlish did not find him so exasperating now; because of this respite the Yard man was again a big, garrulous boy, hiding great shrewdness behind the ponderous speech. 'This is a police inquiry, and you will be well advised not to attempt to make any inquiries yourself.'

Dawlish did not answer.

The motor-scooter was close to the front door, and he could see the girl's clothes out of the corner of his eye. He didn't look round. Penfold said 'Good afternoon' in a pompous way, and King opened the door for him. They went out. Dawlish wiped his forehead with the palm of his hand, and found that it came away wet. There was a murmur of words in the hall, then Ruby Ard arrived, holding a brown carrier bag bulging with food packages in both arms; a milk bottle stuck out at one end of the bag. She looked fresh and attractive, and in spite of the pirate's skullcap her hair was more unruly; it was wiry as well as dark.

Her smile faded.

'My,' she said, 'they gave you a bad time!'

'Does it show like that?' Dawlish asked ruefully.

'You look as if you've been steam-rollered,' Ruby told him, 'and you also look as if you'd like to wring the neck of the next man you see.'

'That's about right.' It was difficult to relish her frankness.

'How many Penfolds are there?' Ruby asked, with a grimace, then turned towards the hall. 'This one may have spoiled your appetite, but I'm ravenous.'

'It takes a lot to kill my appetite,' Dawlish said, but that was only half true. It was not only what Penfold had told him, not only the apparent evidence that someone was trying to make him look guilty, and was drawing very close to success; it was the fact that he had shown the effect of that police questioning so clearly. He was not really on top of himself; it was as if the police had the skids under him, and were determined to keep them there.

'Does your wife hate any other woman messing about in her kitchen?' Ruby asked. She put the groceries down carefully on the table, then began to unpack the bag. 'Some women don't, I know. Will you unpack these things while I cut those sandwiches? I'm not much use at anything except boiling eggs and cutting bread-and-butter, and then only if the butter's soft.' She was talking for the sake of talking, and saving Dawlish the need of replying. He soon felt in better spirits, and the sight of the crusty loaf being sliced expertly, and the sight of large juicy-looking pieces of ham going between the slices, did him good. He put a kettle on, fetched plates, knives and forks, and found that Ruby had brought a large tin of fruit and a small pot of cream. For the first time since Penfold had gone, he found himself smiling.

'I intended to do myself proud,' Ruby declared.

'Provided you do me proud too, that's fine.'

Ruby looked up at him, as if she was glad to hear the lighter note in his voice.

'Was he really a devil?' she asked.

'If he was right,' Dawlish said carefully, 'someone is trying to get me hanged for the murder of your sister, and she was being used to make me fall into the trap.'

'Oh, *no.*'

'Oh, yes,' said Dawlish, studying her; and doing so, he wondered whether she was as shocked as she pretended, and reminded himself again of the thought that she would be too easy to trust; as her sister had been. He realised another thing, which he didn't talk about. Ruby was showing remarkable fortitude. Her sister had been found murdered only a day or so ago, and on her own admission she herself was under some kind of suspicion for murder; but none of that really affected her gaiety. Gaiety was the right word, too, although for the moment it was driven out of her eyes.

'How well did you know Marion's friends?' Dawlish asked.

'Well, as a matter of fact I hardly knew Marion,' said Ruby, quietly. She pulled up a chair, opened a sandwich, and began to spread mustard very liberally. 'We were sisters, but that was all—I'm seven years older, I *was* rather, and our parents didn't live together. They weren't divorced, just separated. I lived with my father most of the time, and Marion lived with my mother, who was half Spanish. We never did get on really well, and funnily enough the differences between us were the same as the differences between our parents. My father was a very down-to-earth, practical man, and Mother was—well, Mother was the reverse.' Ruby was talking with the sandwich poised in front of her, her eyes gleamed and flashed, and she illustrated her narration with easy, flowing movements of her left hand. 'Things finally broke up over the ouija board, there were parties and séances and all that kind of nonsense, and Dad was driven out of his mind. So he picked me up by the scruff of the neck, and we left.'

'Where is he now?' asked Dawlish, oddly impressed by the story.

Ruby said: 'He died five years ago. A coronary thrombosis. I keep telling myself I'm over the loss.' She bit into the sandwich. 'My, is this ham good!'

'It's home grown,' Dawlish said.

'What?'

'I keep my own pigs and there's a little curing-plant not far away where they make a real job of the bacon and ham,' Dawlish explained. 'There's also an unwritten understanding that the village shop keeps no ham but Dawlish ham.' He was glad to see her smile, and wondered how deeply the five-year wound really hurt. 'Anything I can get you?'

'I'd love a glass of milk,' Ruby said, suddenly. 'That's how I keep my schoolgirl complexion. Mr Dawlish,' she went on, as he got up and went to the refrigerator for the milk, then collected two glasses from the dresser, 'I have a feeling that Penfold is even more suspicious of you than of me. Did you tell him that you thought you were being framed?'

'No.'

'I suppose that's what you *would* claim, even if you had killed Marion,' observed Ruby, thoughtfully; she looked surprised when Dawlish grinned. 'What's funny? . . . Oh, you'll get used to me calling a spade a spade, that was one of the reasons I could never get on with Marion—or Mother, for that matter. They always wrapped everything up so much, and—but don't misunderstand me, Mr Dawlish, I'm sorry that Marion died, especially in such a beastly way, and I'd do a lot to find out who killed her. Are you going to try to find out, or are you going to leave it to them?'

'Penfold told me that I must leave it to them.'

Her eyes gleamed.

'So you're going to try to find out for yourself! May I help? And don't say no,' she added, 'because whatever you say, I'm going to.' She stopped to finish the first sandwich, drink half her milk, and then pick up another sandwich. 'What do you want me to do?'

'There was a small, dark-haired man with a bald patch watching Marion,' Dawlish told her, and explained about Tim and the fact that there was still no word of him. 'You can find out if any of her friends know this bald-headed man—if her landlady saw the man, for instance, and all the kinds of things that a sister would be expected to want to find out, in the circumstances. Such as—'

'Did she have a boy friend? Did anyone sleep with her? And was it always the same man?' asked Ruby, quite matter-of-factly. 'I'm to behave as if I must at all costs find the devil who killed my sister—and people might talk more freely to me than to you or to the police, isn't that what you think?'

'That's exactly what I think,' agreed Dawlish, and laughed with her. Quite impersonally, her left hand fell upon his, and squeezed and lingered just for a moment. He had time again to notice how cool her fingers were, before she took her hand away.

'And what are you going to do yourself?' Ruby asked briskly.

'My first job is to find Tim,' answered Dawlish.

It was about half past three in the afternoon when Ruby left. Dawlish saw her off as she drove down the drive, bright and gay looking, with the little engine popping. She waved from the foot of the drive. The policeman there and the policeman at the porch could not fail to notice this; and the second man would in due course report the way Dawlish smiled, as if the thought of the girl pleased him.

Dawlish went indoors.

Smith and Harrison had gone, telling him that they had finished at Four Ways, although they might want to come back. The storage-room, empty except for a few cases and some crates and packing material, was sealed up. Dawlish remembered taking that empty trunk into the room, remembered the labels which Felicity had stuck on, forgetting that they would not need the second trunk. What would have happened to Marion Ard's body if they had taken that trunk?

He went into the back garden.

He had already seen Old Josh and questioned him closely without getting anywhere. Josh was cleaning out the fowl-house, which was at the end of the orchard beyond the house itself. He worked placidly, was as brown as any sailor, and had little to say. Dawlish left him, wondering whether he was as indifferent as he seemed, and went back into the house, telling himself that he ought to be glad that he had forced Penfold's hand; at least he knew the worst. Now that he was alone, it seemed more oppressive.

The restriction on his movements was going to cause difficulties, too. If he ignored the warning, the police had enough circumstantial evidence to make an arrest, and could put a call out for him. Whatever he did he had to be careful, and caution in circumstances like these was all against every impulse he had. He looked through the bureau and his own desk, making sure that the letters from Marion were not there. It was a pointless search; the killer had taken those all right. He sat down at the telephone, and put in a call to some friends in London. He had two close friends, besides Tim, but one was abroad, the other was a furiously busy general practitioner.

Neither of the people Dawlish called had seen Tim for days.

He tried their two clubs; Tim had not been seen at either for a week or more.

Dawlish spent nearly an hour on the telephone, and learned nothing at all during it. Tim had left here yesterday morning, and vanished without a trace. Was that a cause for worry? Dawlish refused to let it be. As Tim had sent that radiogram, he would expect Dawlish home by now, and was sure to come or to telephone soon, but Dawlish had a caged feeling; action was the thing he craved.

More; he began to worry in case Tim had run into trouble.

He tried to put that thought out of his mind.

The house was guarded, for no better reason than to keep an eye on him. A few sightseers gathered at the gate from time to time, and the police moved them on, so they were not entirely useless. At a quarter past five, Dawlish drove to Haslemere and picked up newspapers for the past week; they had been obtained from a wholesaler specially for him. He read every word about the finding of Marion Ard's body, and it wasn't pleasant. His own photographs kept staring at him, so did the dead girl's. She photographed well; her eyes had a soulful, innocent look, as of a child. Between the lines was the story which had gradually been built up against him, Dawlish; the 'coincidence' of his going to South Africa; the fact that the police were in touch with the shipping company; the fact that he was on his way home, and might come by air. One newspaper suggested that Scotland Yard officers were to fly to Cairo to interview him. No one who read these stories could be in much doubt that the police thought him guilty of murder. The only question they made no attempt to answer was why he should leave the body in a trunk in his own home.

If there were a prosecution, the police would find some reasonable explanation to present to a jury. Perhaps that was the present weakness in the case, the reason why he was not yet under arrest.

Dawlish had another worry.

There was a risk that Felicity would see some of these newspapers, for editions would be flown out to Cairo, and someone would take copies on board. If she saw them while the ship was in port, she would almost certainly try to fly home; if she didn't see them until the ship was at sea again, she would have to stay aboard, for Cairo was the last port of call.

These things kept going through his mind, together with the persistent question: who would want him blamed for this crime?

He might have been selected because Marion Ard had appealed to him for help. Some of the facts which Penfold had told him made this theory difficult to accept, but it remained a possibility: that whoever had set out to kill Marion had wanted

69

to point the finger of guilt at someone else, and had selected him. If that were the case, it was like fighting the air; he had nowhere to start from, no indication of the best place to look for the killer.

But could the killer come out of his own past?

Now was the time to stand back and look at himself and the many men whom he had fought and damned. Then it had been high adventure, later it had become almost a vocation, as with the police. But in the prisons of this country there must be twenty men, still serving long sentences, whom he had put there.

Some of these would hate him.

Others might have come out of prison during the past few months, or even the past few years. That was a line he could follow; find out who, having cause to hate him, had been released from prison.

There was another line to follow, too.

Tim had said that Marion had been alive for two days; he had actually seen her, and seen the man following; had watched her go in and out of her flat. Why had no one else seen her in those two days? Dawlish had to remind himself again that the police would not lie; they might be prejudiced, but they would be just. A curious buoyancy took hold of him from that moment. He had been too harassed, had allowed himself to be pushed around too easily, and could blame that on to the swift transition from tropical heat to English chill, or to the fact that he had been so shaken when he had realised the attitude of the police. All he had to do was to find one person—just one who did not know him but who had seen Marion Ard after he had left England.

That couldn't be impossible.

It had to be done soon.

There was the landlady, the neighbours, the tradespeople,

dozens of people to ask, many who might be persuaded to remember some forgotten trifle of importance. This was a line to follow, he had been blind to it before. And in spite of Penfold, Dawlish knew that he would make the inquiries himself; he could not stay here doing nothing.

It might even lead to Tim.

Dawlish jumped up from an armchair in the drawing-room, went across to a cabinet and picked up a bottle of whisky. It had a clip-on cap. He flicked this open, a little square of white curved an arc through the air, and dropped on the cocktail cabinet.

It had been inside the cap of the whisky bottle, quite invisible.

'Tim!' he exclaimed, and his eyes glinted as he picked up the paper, a tiny wad compressed so tightly that it was like thin card-board. He glanced out of the window, in case a policeman was watching; none was nearer than fifty yards. He turned his back on the window, then began to pick at the sides, to loosen and unfold it. It was so tight that he kept tearing the paper slightly, and he began to wonder if he could open without destroying it; then to fear that Felicity had put this here, to keep the bottle tightly capped.

He unfolded it twice, until it was slightly larger than a postage stamp, still folded tightly; but now it was easier to open, and he picked up one corner with his finger nail.

He saw the marks of a pencil.

'It's Tim all right,' he said with deep relief. He sat on the arm of a big chair and continued to unfold it, seeing more and more writing; and when it was completely open he recognised Tim's writing.

His grin could not have been broader.

The dam' fools think you did it (Tim wrote). *They're trying to prove that you've known her for months. That's the danger, lying witnesses.*

I'm going hunting until you're back, but I'll soon be in touch. Can't do any of the known haunts, Penfold knows them all—or can find out. I do not like Mr P. Don't trust him. Don't trust Mrs Wattle, the landlady at M. A.'s place, either; think she's being blackmailed to lie about you. Watch her. If Fel's back, love.

Dawlish put the letter down.

Tim would not hunt unless he had some specific quarry in mind; so Tim had done him more good than a dozen whiskies and sodas. And Tim had told him a lot: if the police found any witness who would lie by swearing that Dawlish and the girl had known each other for months, or even weeks, then the police would almost certainly have their case.

Were there any lying witnesses?

That landlady?

'The quicker I go and see her the better,' Dawlish said aloud.

He looked out at the cloudless blue of the evening sky, and went on: 'The damned daylight lasts so long at this time of the year, it won't be dark until after ten. Anyhow, where can I pick up a car?'

It did not occur to him to think twice about leaving here without telling the police. That was a chance he had to take, for he had to see that landlady, and had to see her soon.

9

JOURNEY BY NIGHT

It was very dark, not quite pitch, for the stars were out, but there was no moon. Dawlish, standing at the bedroom window, with the light on behind him and with his pyjamas open at the neck, looked out at the silent garden. Now and again, he heard a man cough. At the far end of the drive there was a red glow, brighter at times than others: Chief Inspector Smith probably did not know that his men smoked when on night duty. Beyond was the light of a distant house, two miles away at least.

Dawlish yawned loudly, then turned away and put out the light.

He actually got into bed.

He lay still for a few minutes, hearing the footsteps of the man on duty close to the house; then he heard the scrape of a match. That suggested a policeman in a relaxed frame of mind. Very cautiously, he sat up and got out of bed. He stripped off the pyjama jacket and untucked the open-necked shirt he wore beneath it. He buttoned this up, slipped on a tie, then put on a pair of old rubber-soled shoes. He drew on a pair of thin cotton gloves, then put a scarf round his neck and put on a small cloth cap. Next, he tip-toed out of the bedroom, across the landing, and to the back of the house. There was a spare room over the kitchen, and he had opened the window earlier. Just outside was the porch of the back door, the easiest place to climb out.

A man was on duty at the back.

Nothing could have made it more clear that Dawlish was under grave suspicion; but now he leaned against the wall by the open window, smoking a cigarette, waiting for the moment when the man on duty would take a stroll. There was a soft whistle, as from the side of the house; and another, from below. The waiting man here moved into sight, going towards the corner where he would meet the man at the front.

Dawlish climbed out of the window.

For a moment he was angled against the star-speckled sky, and would be seen if either man glanced his way; then he bent down, out of sight. The slanting roof hid him from the corner. He heard the man begin to talk in the monotonous undertone of caution. Gradually, he edged himself towards the guttering, and as gradually lowered himself so that soon he was hanging full length. He was only an inch or so from the ground. He landed silently, hidden by the porch; the only danger if the man from the drive had come up here.

Dawlish went stealthily towards the corner opposite the two policemen. Any sound now would bring them running. He reached the corner and peered round, but there was only the darkness of the garden leading to the drive. He went across a gravel path, holding his breath, as if that would lighten his great weight. Then he reached grass, and safety. He went straight across to the brick wall which surrounded this part of the garden, knowing that there was a meadow on the other side, with a footpath across it. He hauled himself up and over, then dropped down into long, soft grass; the only sound was a rustle.

He grinned as he turned and walked alongside the wall, then past his orchard, which was separated from the meadowland only by a wire fence. At the top of the rise he could look down and see the lights of villages many miles off and, much nearer, the yellow square of a small window. He walked towards this. A great figure rose out of the earth just in front of him, making him start, and he heard the rustling and the grumbling of a cow he had disturbed. He made a beeline for that lighted window until it was only fifty or sixty yards away; he could see the shape of the farmhouse he was heading for.

This was owned by an old neighbour and an old friend, Tom Mellish.

Mellish had a car here, but if Dawlish used a piece of wire and switched on the ignition and started off, Mellish would come rushing; and he would report immediately that his car had been stolen.

Was he a reliable friend, in spite of what had happened?

He was a middle-aged man, and a bachelor. A man and woman lived in the other side of the house: Mellish's housekeeper and cowman. They had tongues which would never stop chattering, so Dawlish must not ring the bell or bang the knocker.

He reached the window.

A curtain was drawn carelessly, not enough to hide Mellish, who sat in a winged armchair, legs up on another chair, pipe in mouth, glasses on. He was apparently listening to soft music from a record player, and was not on the alert.

Dawlish moved away.

He knew the farmyard and the grounds of the house thoroughly. The drive sloped, and if he could push Mellish's big Austin out of the garage and to the top of the drive, then he could get in, and coast down fifty yards or so away. From there the starting of an engine would not really surprise Mellish, who would probably assume that lovers had selected his fields for the evening's delight.

Dawlish went cautiously round to the garage.

His chief worry was Mellish's dog, a collie which could wake the dead. But he knew the dog well, and was known in turn. He heard it whimper, and was sure that he had been recognised. He saw the outline of the kennel, went to it, and stayed with the dog for a few seconds; it frisked at the end of its long chain.

He left it and went to the garage.

Mellish had closed but not locked it. The doors creaked as Dawlish opened them, but no light appeared at the farmhouse, and he heard no other sound. There was just room between the car and the wall for him to squeeze, and he went in front of the car and began to push. The brakes weren't on, and he had little trouble in getting it halfway out of the garage. Then he had to push from the driving door, so as to guide the car to the top of the drive. Here was the time of greatest danger, for the drive was surfaced with gravel, and the heavy old Austin made a lot of noise. It was useless to drag it out, so he pushed quickly, straining until he felt the car beginning to run away from him. He leaned inside and put on the brake, then stood very still, looking at the one light which was on at the house.

He heard nothing but a quiet wind.

He took the wheel, coasted down without the headlamps, reached the foot of the drive and started the engine without difficulty, then turned into the side road which led to Guildford. It was ten minutes before he switched the lights on.

If he could get the car back as simply as he had brought it away, no one would suspect that he had left his house. Certainly no one would be able to prove it, even if he left the car at the foot of the drive.

His thin cotton gloves made sure there were no fingerprints anywhere. The police at Four Ways might see the headlights but it would not give them a moment's qualm.

Once on the road, Dawlish put his foot down, and the car shot along. He drove through Guildford at a sedate thirty-five, then opened the throttle again. London was a little more than an hour away, and it would be after midnight before he reached the house in Kensington; he had to be back here before dawn.

That gave him no more than four hours.

He felt much more himself now that he was actually doing something; and the measure of risk in being out here had a heady, not a depressing, effect. He had felt buoyant from the time he had seen Tim's letter, and he would soon feel on top of the world.

He drove through the lighted streets of the outskirts of London. Now and again a car passed him on the way to the suburbs; very little traffic was going the same way as he. He reached Chelsea, and ran into Kensington. A few more people were about, and every now and again he saw a policeman. He remembered exactly where the house was, in Harven Street, not far from Gloucester Road, and he went to an adjoining street where some cars were parked without lights. He left the Austin near a corner, and got out.

Even with no one about, he felt conspicuous; this was a time when his height and size made danger. He reached the corner of Harven Street, half expecting to see someone on guard outside, but saw no one. He did not go straight along on the side where Marion Ard had lived but walked along the other side, shoulders bent a little, and throwing his right foot, so that he did not look so noticeably tall. He neared the doorway of a house opposite Marion's, and saw a man sitting in the porch, silent, shadowy, smoking. Did all policemen smoke at night?

Dawlish passed.

The house was being watched, perhaps because Penfold expected him to try to see Mrs Wattle; for Penfold would know that, by Dawlish's arguments, the landlady must have seen the girl alive after he had left the country.

Penfold would not do a job by halves; he would have the back of the house watched, as well. The massive might of the Yard was in action, and it would crush anyone who came in direct conflict with it; Penfold meant it to crush him.

Dawlish reached the far corner.

He stood and looked back along the street, able to pick out the house he wanted because it was almost opposite a street light; and the light seemed very bright. Unless he attacked the watching detective, and so laid himself open to a serious charge, he could not get into that house by the front or by the back.

He looked upwards.

Could he get in by the top?

10

TOP OF THE HOUSE

The safest way to climb was at the back, so that no latecomers and no police patrolling the streets would be likely to see him. Harven Street was a long terrace of houses, with gardens backing on to the fenced gardens of the houses where he had left his car. The first moment of danger came when he climbed the wall of the end garden. He heard footsteps, and waited by the wall; a man and a girl turned into the street. A long way off, Dawlish saw a wavering light, probably of a bicycle. He turned back a few paces, ran, and leapt for the ten-foot wall; he missed the top by inches. He tried again, seeing the wobbling light a little nearer; there would not be time for a third chance.

He began to run.

He heard a car engine start up, with alarming clatter, and nearly checked his run, but he made the leap, clutched the top of the wall, and hauled himself up and over. He dropped down behind the wall as the headlights of a car turned the corner; he could see them shining on the windows of nearby houses. The car passed, and Dawlish turned and studied the backs of the houses, his eyes quite used to the darkness.

Between each garden was a four-foot wall; they would give no trouble. At the back of each pair of houses was a kind of outhouse, probably a scullery or wash-house; each had a chimney. Above these outhouses were three sets of windows and the eaves of the roof.

The roofs were sloping.

Several windows were brightly lit at the back, and a door opened, light streamed out not far along, and a man began to call: '*Bick, Bick, Bick, Bick,*' in a subdued voice. Then came a scuffle, a 'Good dog', and the light was blotted out. Dawlish climbed four garden walls, twice stepping deeply into the soil of a flower or vegetable bed. The gardeners would be agog next morning, and would curse him for any damage he did; but, worse than that, he would leave footprints; and his was a very large foot. It would be wise to destroy these shoes.

At a house halfway along the back of Harven Street he stopped. No lights were near here. He could smell the wood-smoke of a smouldering garden fire, but heard nothing. He went to the outhouse, climbed to the roof without difficulty, then hauled himself to the first window-sill. The blind was drawn at the window, and he did not think there was much to worry about. He hauled himself up to the second window fairly easily, until he was standing on the sill. He had made very little noise, but even his own breathing sounded loud.

He stretched up for the next window, which was more difficult.

It was just within reach of his fingers when he stood on tiptoe.

He got the tips of his fingers on to the rough sill, and began to haul himself up; the strain on his fingers and knuckles was excruciating. He was sweating when at last he managed to get the whole of one hand flat on the sill and steady himself. He went up gradually, muscles bulging, veins standing out on his neck and forehead, teeth clenched so tightly that his jaws hurt. He scuffled the wall a little, and could not avoid making some noise. If anyone was sleeping in the room beyond, he might wake them; and if an alarm were raised he would have no chance to get up or down.

At last, he was squatting on the window-sill

No blind was drawn here, and the window was open; there was still a risk that he would be seen, but he had to stand up here, and reach for the roof; at least that was within easy reach. He put his face near the window, trying to see in; and he saw a sleeping child close to the window, mouth open slightly, arms crooked above its head.

Dawlish grinned. . . .

As he climbed over the slate roofs, crouching low to make sure that he was not clearly visible, he heard a clock strike and chime; it was half past twelve. He was on the street side of the houses now, watching for the one with the lamp outside and the man in the porch opposite. He saw the man first, lighting a cigarette as he strolled up and down. Dawlish kept quite still until the man passed, and had his back to him for a moment. Then Dawlish crossed the angled roof again, and began to lower himself over the guttering to the window-sill of a room in Mrs Wattle's house.

There were several flatlets here, and he did not want to get into one of them; a bathroom would be safer. The danger of being here, measured against the slim chance he had of getting anything that would help, had suddenly become very vivid. But he peered over, saw a bedroom window and close to it a narrower window open at the top; that was what he wanted. It was within easy reach; he need only lean over the guttering to push the window open wider—provided the man at the back did not notice him.

He lay spreadeagled on the roof, stretching down, imagining what would happen if the window squeaked. He pushed cautiously, and it moved without a sound; soon he had it as wide open as necessary.

Now he had to lower himself until he was standing on the sill, and climb through.

He prayed that no watching man would be looking up here.

He was standing on a small W.C., staring out of the window. He could just make out the figure of the watching man.

There was just a possibility that Penfold would have a man inside this house, but Dawlish did not think it likely. He opened the door on to a narrow passage; a low-wattage lamp gave an eerie yellow impression, but he was grateful for any light. He reached the end of the passage and looked down a narrow flight of stairs, the linoleum shining unexpectedly. There was no sound. He pressed himself against the wall and started down, a step at a time; and even though he trod as lightly as he could, the boards creaked; if anyone was awake, they would certainly hear. He reached the next landing, and more shiny yellowy-brown linoleum and another wider flight of stairs. Two doors led off here, one of them to the room where Marion Ard had taken him. He stared at the door, half expecting to see it sealed off, but it was not. Had the room been let again? He went past it, down stairs which creaked much less, and soon reached Flat 1. The number, in faded black on a brown door, showed up clearly in the yellow light, and the name, Mrs Wattle, was on a printed card; he had seen it when he had come here with Marion Ard.

It was an ordinary, old-fashioned lock.

Dawlish took out a skeleton key which he had used often enough in the past. The sound of metal on metal seemed very loud. It took a long time, too; was he becoming less expert, or was he jittery? He felt the key catch the lock, twisted, and heard the lock click back. He stood inside, watching the front door and this door, and listening intently; but nothing suggested that he had been heard.

He opened the door.

Here was darkness.

He left the door ajar, and the light which had seemed so pale before seemed very bright now, showing up the big furniture and reflecting from a wide mirror over a sideboard. This room had a musty smell, too.

He saw a closed door, and an open one. He stepped to the open one, and found himself in a kitchen; a bathroom led off it. He went to the window, and studied the curtains; they seemed drawn closely enough, but the detective was watching on the other side of the street.

Dawlish drew a pencil torch from his pocket, and shone it round, avoiding the window. Then he went into the next room, the door of which was ajar. The beam of light fell upon an old-fashioned davenport, with some letters standing on it. He went across and tried the lid; it was not locked. Inside was a mass of papers, some old books, pens and pencils; this had not been tidied for months.

He had a sickening feeling that he would find nothing here; that the urge for swift action had driven him into a mistake which might be fatal. If he were found here, Penfold would act ruthlessly. He turned back to the papers and picked up a book with a shiny black cover, and the words *Rent Book* written on a piece of white sticking paper, a corner of which was rolled up. There was one name for every few pages and on each page the number of a flat. He looked for 'Flat 3, Marion Ard'; she had been in the flat for two years, and had always paid her rent promptly; date due and date paid were always the same. Mrs Wattle wasn't always so lucky with her tenants. Three had been frequently in arrears for three or four weeks, and she had carefully noted promises, in pencil, such as: '*Promised* 2 *weeks next week*, 2 *weeks the following w*.' Others had got over four weeks in arrears, and in bright red was the comment: '*Given Notice*.' New tenants had come in almost immediately afterwards, a pointer to the difficulty of getting accommodation in London.

Dawlish turned a page, on the point of thinking: 'There'll be nothing here.'

This was in the name of a man, a Bertram Hillman, in Flat 4. At first, Hillman had paid regularly; then he had started paying in arrears, and the usual remarks had been placed on his page. Four months ago he seemed to have stopped paying altogether and there was no 'Given notice' comment. Nor was there any other named tenant in Flat 4.

Well, what was so remarkable?

There could be an *affaire* between landlady and lodger, when such sordid details as rent were overlooked. But there could also be pressure to bear, compelling Mrs Wattle to allow the man to live rent free, just as there appeared to have been pressure brought to bear to make Mrs Wattle say that she had not seen Marion Ard on those two fateful days.

Dawlish rummaged through the papers. There were several notes which made it obvious that Hillman still lived here. The only other thing which caught Dawlish's eye were bills for beer and spirits from a public-house he had often noticed on the other side of the Thames because of its name—the Pack of Lies. That had no significance as far as he knew.

Then he came upon a pencilled note, carelessly folded and stuck down one side of the davenport; in a big, schoolboyish hand, it said:

The address is Four Ways, Alum, Nr. Haslemere, Surrey. Telephone Alum 41.

Dawlish felt his jaws tensing with excitement. There was no date, nothing to indicate when it had been written, but the folds were so uneven and criss-crossed and the paper so crumpled that it was obviously some time since it had been written. Now he unfolded one piece of paper after another, until he came upon one in the same handwriting. This said simply:

I'll be away for a few days, expect me when you see me. Bert.

Bert for Bertram.

Bert, who no longer paid Mrs Wattle any rent, had written the Alum address down—for her, or for Marion Ard. Even the police would admit that this was peculiar but there was no way of reporting it to them without taking the risk that they would know how he had obtained it. He mustn't blot his copybook with the police any more while he was just one step from arrest.

He wanted urgently to talk with Bertram Hillman, and Mrs Wattle.

And the woman was in the next room.

Dawlish stepped towards the closed door, turned the handle very softly, and stood with the door ajar. He could hear even breathing, of a man or woman; and after a moment he was sure that only one person was in here. So Mrs Wattle didn't always share her bed with Hillman, if she shared it at all. Dawlish opened the door wider, and light fell upon the foot of the bed, the head of which was behind the door. He could just make out the outline of the woman's head and shoulders, clearly enough to see that she wore an old-fashioned hair-net which seemed to hold her hair in a basket. There was a smell of scent, and the last thing he would have expected, for Felicity used scent like this. Dawlish wasn't sure what it was called, but undoubtedly it was good and expensive. Did Mrs Wattle treat herself to expensive perfumes and cosmetics? If so, where did she get the money? From the rents?

Dawlish pushed the scarf up over his nose and pulled the cap down over his eyes, located the light switch of the bedside lamp, then went into the room. Slowly and gently he placed a hand over the sleeping woman's mouth. She started convulsively, awake on the instant. He saw her terror, as she tried desperately to shout. Dawlish pressed harder, so that all she could make were gulping sounds. Even in this poor light, he could see the gleam of her frightened eyes. She tried to hitch herself up in the bed, but he prevented her. She was big, soft and flabby, and began to tremble like a jelly.

'If you do what you're told, I won't hurt you,' Dawlish said. 'What hold has Hillman got over you?'

She kept shivering, even when he eased the pressure of his hand, so as to give her time to answer. He would know at once if she was going to try to shout, she would take a deep breath first. She must be in abject terror, with a huge shadowy shape looming over her, and that powerful hand against her lips; terrified, she might be more likely to answer.

'Come on,' Dawlish said roughly. 'What's Hillman got on you? What made you lie about Marion Ard? You saw her here but told the police you hadn't. How did Hillman make you lie?'

He eased the pressure again.

She gasped: 'He said he'd kill me. I had to do it; he said he'd kill me.'

11

NEW TARGET

Dawlish felt the woman's breath hot on the palm of his hand as she gasped the answer, too frightened even to make a denial. And ten minutes ago he had thought it a wasted journey. Now that she had made the admission, she wasn't likely to shout for help; she would realise that she had committed herself too far.

Dawlish took his hand away.

'So Marion Ard was here until June 1st?'

'Yes, yes, she—she was ever so nervous; I told her she would have to go, she was scaring me with her stories, but I'—the frightened woman gabbled I-I-I-I a dozen times, and then blurted out: 'I didn't know they were going to kill her!'

'Why did Hillman make you lie to the police?'

'I dunno!'

That was probably the truth; that Hillman had some hold over her and could make her do whatever he wanted, but the nature of the hold did not greatly matter. The only important thing was the fact that she had lied. There must be a way of making her admit it to the police. Supposing he called them now, admitting that he had broken in and letting them hear her admission while she was still frightened?

They would say that the admission had been obtained under duress, of course, and no court would permit it as evidence. He had to be much more cunning. A signed confession note would probably serve, and he believed that he could make this woman sign one. Later she would probably try to retract, saying that she had signed the note under pressure, but a signed admission would be bound to help. She had lied to the police because she had been frightened, and she would do what Dawlish wanted only if she were frightened more of him than of Hillman.

'Did anyone else see Marion Ard on those two days?' he demanded.

'I don't know,' she muttered.

'Did Hillman?'

'Yes! He knew she was okay, he—'

She broke off, still terrified, and Dawlish did not think that there was any further need to fear her.

That was the moment when he heard the sound in the other room.

Dawlish did not know whether the woman heard it or not; her fear might deafen her. It was only a click, as of a door being closed very gently. He stood up, making Mrs Wattle cringe back on her pillow.

'If you make a sound, I'll choke the life out of you,' he whispered, and sounded as if he meant it. He stared at the door, and fancied that he could pick out the shape of a man coming slowly into the room. He spoke as if he was still bending over the woman, but keeping his voice low. 'Who else saw Marion Ard besides you and Hillman? Come on, out with it.'

'I don't know,' she gasped, and then she raised her voice and cried. '*Bert!*'

The door swung open, and light flooded the room.

A small, thin-faced man, wearing a red dressing-gown, eyes glittering, right arm raised and with an iron bar in it, jumped forward. Had Dawlish not heard that click, he would not have stood a chance. As it was, he thrust out a hand and brushed the other's arm aside, then struck him savagely on the nose.

Hillman dodged back, gasping with pain; but he kept his balance. The iron bar was still clutched tightly in his right hand, nothing suggested that he would be easy to overcome.

The woman was scrambling out of bed, a flurry of frills and fat legs.

Hillman tried to smash another blow at Dawlish, who thrust his hand up, caught the man's wrist between thumb and fore-finger, and jerked it upwards. The weapon flew out of Hillman's grasp. There was a sharp, frightening explosion, making Mrs Wattle scream. Dawlish knew what had happened, after the first shock: the iron bar had struck the electric lamp bulb. Now the damage had been done; there was the explosion, the scream, the thudding noises as Hillman staggered away and banged into a chair; and that crashed against something which clattered and echoed about the room.

The detective in the street could not fail to hear the din; he would be halfway across the road already.

Dawlish heard a police whistle.

The light from the outer room showed Hillman getting to his feet, and the woman on the other side of the bed, standing upright. She looked like a dressed-up doll in her night-bonnet and her frilly nightdress with its deep V. She was wheezing and gasping and quivering.

The only hope was to get out by the roof, and that chance wouldn't remain for long, soon the whole area be cordoned off. Dawlish strode into the outer room, and closed the door behind him. The door leading to the passage was open, but the passage light was on. He reached that doorway and started for the stairs; as he did so, he heard Mrs Wattle scream again.

That startled him.

Was she hysterical, now that he had gone?

The police whistle shrilled out, there was a thumping at the front door, and the bell rang loudly inside the house. Racing up the stairs, he saw a light go on under the door of one of the flats, but the door didn't open. He swung round to the next flight of stairs, footsteps thudding, staircase so creaky that he felt almost as if he would break them down. He reached the third landing; now there was only that very narrow flight of stairs leading to the top passage, the toilet, and the window leading to the roof. The policeman at the back would have heard the first shrill whistle; his was probably going, and within minutes patrol cars would be in the street.

If Dawlish had five minutes' grace, he would be lucky.

He saw the door of the W.C. closed, had a fleeting thought that he had left it open, grabbed the handle, twisted and pushed: and the door wouldn't budge. *Had Hillman locked it?* If he tried to break it down, he would attract attention, and would not have even a minute's time.

He must reach a window he could climb through.

There were two others, one from the room on his right, one from the room on his left, but both doors were closed, both almost certainly locked. Short of smashing the other door down, he hadn't a chance; and he realised it then. A surge of wild thoughts went through his mind: to race downstairs and force his way out of the front door; or out of the back, he could tackle three or even four men at a time. All he had to do was run round to the borrowed Austin, and get away; but within minutes a radio call would be out, every car in the vicinity would be stopped by the police.

'The truth is,' he said in a clear voice, 'that I haven't a chance in hell.'

There was still the thudding on the front door, but the sound of the police whistle had stopped. He thought he heard banging on the back door. A moment later, there came a thump of footsteps, and the sound of a car engine not far away. A draught of cool air swept up the well of the staircase.

He drew back, thrusting his weight against the bathroom door. It creaked and seemed to sag. He threw himself forward again, and one of the hinges broke, but did not pull right away from the door. At the third attempt he would have the door down, but already the police would be watching the roof.

He drew back.

A door opened, and a woman stood in the doorway, clearly visible in the yellow light.

It was Ruby Ard.

She recognised Dawlish because of his size, of course; no one who knew him could have any serious doubt. She stood with a hand on the door, darkness beyond her, wearing a pair of loose-fitting pyjamas; that was all he noticed, except that her dark hair was loose about her shoulders, picking out the light. Downstairs, voices were raised and words were distinguishable.

'Where is he?'

'Upstairs.'

'Get after him.'

'Better flash the Yard.'

Men would be at the first landing by now. The fight was all over, and the only chance he had won out of this night's madness was that Mrs Wattle might be made to tell the truth. His own defending counsel would be merciless with her, would surely be able to break her down.

Ruby said: 'You can hide in here,' and stood aside.

She did not put on the light, even when she closed the door. The footsteps of the coming men were on the flight of stairs below, and no one could have seen this door open, or heard her words; and the thumping probably drowned the sound of this door closing. The only light was pale grey, from the stars. Dawlish felt her hands close about his arm, then felt the pressure of her cool body.

'In bed,' she whispered. 'Get under the clothes.'

She pushed him. He felt the edge of the bed against the back of his knees. He felt, hopelessly, that it was a waste of time, and would only involve her, for he was the last person to be able to lie concealed in a single bed.

'Hurry,' she whispered. 'There's a gap between the bed and the wall.'

He found himself crouching on the bed, with the springs creaking. He wriggled down. Now, men were coming up the stairs, and someone called: 'Watch the roof. Is there a loft?' Dawlish was under the bedclothes when a light went on in this room, and Ruby whispered:

'I'll sit up in bed, and pretend—'

He did not hear what else she said, but poked his head out of the bedclothes, and saw what she meant by 'a gap'. The bed was perhaps a foot from the wall. He could lower his legs over the side, the lower half of his body would be squeezed between the bed and the wall, and the rumpled bedclothes might then be sufficient camouflage. He wriggled down. There were more voices, then a bang on this door. Ruby didn't answer. There was another bang, and she called out as if in a scared voice:

'Who's that?'

'Police, miss. Open the door, please.'

She sat down on the side of the bed; Dawlish felt it sag under her weight.

'Open the door, miss, please, in the name of the law.'

'How—do I know you're the police?'

'No need to worry,' another man called. 'Just open the door, please.'

'Just a moment,' Ruby called.

Dawlish felt her pushing clothes back, and knew that she was giving him every possible chance. As he breathed the hot air beneath the clothes, he realised that she was taking an almost ludicrous risk.

This wasn't the time to *think*.

Dawlish could hear the voices, but did not hear her open the door. He did feel a slight trembling as men walked into the room. He thought that one went to the window, the other to a corner where he had noticed a wardrobe. There was a sound that might have been the creaking of the wardrobe door.

'What's happened? What are you looking for?' Ruby asked. The bedclothes muffled the shrillness of her voice.

'We're looking for a man who broke into the house.'

'But he couldn't have come in here,' she protested, and Dawlish did not know whether to pray that she should not overdo it, or to applaud her nerve. 'I was asleep, some banging woke me.'

'It's all right, miss,' a man said, 'there's no need to worry. We had to look everywhere.'

'Who was the man?'

'All we know for certain is that he's a big fellow,' the speaker said, 'but you needn't worry. Lock your door again, and forget about it. Sorry we disturbed you.'

'I couldn't possibly *sleep* after that,' Ruby protested shrilly.

The men went out. Dawlish pushed the bedclothes up, and

gulped in cool air. 'Just lock your door again,' one of the men called in that heavily reassuring tone.

Dawlish believed that Ruby Ard went on to the landing after them. He heard a door crash, then a window open with a bang. He could imagine that they were already climbing on to the roof, feeling sure that he had escaped the way he had come in. If the police found a closed window, though, they would know that he was still in the house. He heard another mumble of voices, then heard a man shout, loudly, and there seemed an edge of alarm in his voice.

The door of this room closed firmly.

He pushed the bedclothes further back, but didn't get out of bed. The door was not locked, of course, and he was ready to duck out of sight the moment there was a sound outside. He wished that he could hear what was being said, but, with the door closed, was not even sure that men were near the room. He took deep breaths and stared at the door, listening intently, but already beginning to ask himself questions, especially one about Ruby Ard.

What was she doing in this house?

It wasn't the address she had given him.

And why had she offered him sanctuary?

Then he heard a sound outside, and ducked out of sight again.

12

NEW SHOCK

Dawlish thought that he heard the door open and close, but did not move until the bedclothes were pushed back, and Ruby said: 'It's all right, the door's locked.' The whisper just penetrated the channel made by the sheet which covered him. He eased himself up in the bed, and saw her standing and staring with those penetrating clear blue eyes. There was a speculative gleam in them, and a hint of a smile on her face. She looked very fresh and clear-skinned without make-up, and her skin was not greased. The dark hair, hanging to her shoulders, framed her face and made her look very pale; and the pallor made the blue of her eyes even more vivid.

'Speak in whispers,' she advised.

'Believe me I will!'

Her smile became wider, obviously she was laughing at him. Who could blame her? He must look ridiculous, half in and half out of the bed, wearing day-time clothes, and with his scarf hanging round his neck. As he pushed the bedclothes further back, he caught sight of his cap, and drew it out.

She stifled a laugh.

'*Quiet,*' Dawlish breathed, and tried to join her with silent laughter. But he was too alert and edgy for the sound of the men outside.

Ruby did not ask him why he was here; she was quite a remarkable young woman, and undoubtedly set out to make that obvious. Dawlish now sat up on the far side of the bed, legs dangling to the floor, back against the wall, not at all uncomfortable. Ruby sat on the other side, and put her feet up. The legs of her pyjamas rucked nearly to the knees. She had beautiful slender legs, less pale than her face because of slight sun-tan. The white of her ankles was almost transparent, and only the shadowiest of blue veins showed.

She tucked a pillow behind her back.

'So you decided to come and see Mrs Wattle, too,' she observed.

'You had the same idea, did you?'

'Oh, yes, weeks ago,' said Ruby. 'When Marion had been missing for three weeks, I came along to talk to Mrs Wattle, and decided that she was the most dishonest old hag I'd ever seen. Have you ever seen her by day?'

'No.'

'There's the familiar saying, mutton dressed up as lamb,' said Ruby, leaning her head against the wall and smiling at him, 'and that's Ma Wattle to a T. She's sixty-five if she's a day, and must have had her face lifted twice. She uses rouge and powder as if she were a whore, and wears clothes that are far too young for me. She also dyes her hair—bright auburn! I will say,' Ruby added, 'that she has a remarkably fine head of hair. If she only had the sense to let it stay grey, she would look almost human.'

'Why the pronouncement on Mrs Wattle?' inquired Dawlish. 'Are you trying to soothe my nerves?'

'Don't they need it?'

'You've already done it.'

'Thank you, sir.' She was almost skittish, and Dawlish did not understand that; unless it was the effect of a kind of excitement. Her cheeks were more flushed than they had been, and those beautiful eyes were brilliant. 'I just thought you'd like to know what Ma was like. When I first saw her I felt sure she was lying about Marion, there was something so shifty about her, but you know how it is with some people, they look such liars that you don't believe them even when they're telling the truth. I couldn't understand where Marion was, at the time, and thought that if I lived in the same house I might learn more about what she's been doing, but I have to admit it didn't amount to much. She seems to have led a pleasant enough life, with her knitting-machine and her customers. The thing I most wanted to find out was when she began to be frightened.'

'Did you find out?'

'Yes,' said Ruby, and her smile vanished. 'According to some neighbours, it was three or four months ago.'

'About the time that a certain Mr Hillman started to live here, rent free,' said Dawlish, straight-faced.

Ruby almost gasped. 'You *know* that?'

'Hush!'

'Sorry. But—have you been in Mrs W.'s room?'

'Yes.'

'I can understand why Marion thought her troubles would be over if she persuaded you to help!'

'How well do you know Hillman?' Dawlish asked.

'Hardly at all,' admitted Ruby. 'I thought that he might fall for my charms, but he's remained impervious, which I think must indicate a guilty conscience. He's a short, rather ugly little man, and I'm sure that he can't afford to be too choosy in his love life.'

Dawlish thought. 'I wonder just what does go on in your mind.'

She was being deliberately flippant, of course, and he was not quite sure why, although the possibility that it was due to excitement remained. She was still flushed, her eyes were very bright, and she certainly had a look of excitement. 'I'd almost given up hope of finding out anything from Hillman or Ma W.,' she went on. 'Did you find anything else?'

'Only that she lied to the police about not seeing Marion on the last day of May and the first of June, and that Hillman compelled her to lie.'

'You're *sure*?'

'She told me so under some persuasion, and I think that she'll crack under Counsel's pressure, if it ever gets so far.'

'So that lets you out.' Ruby did not show pleasure or regret.

'If I'm caught here by the police, and they can prove that I broke in here—which they can—I'll be in much deeper than ever,' Dawlish said. It was a strain to keep whispering, but he dared not raise his voice. His mouth was dry, and he kept moistening his lips with his tongue. 'I shall be shown to the world as a great ugly brute who forced his way into a defenceless woman's room, and tried to make her lie to save his life for committing a nasty murder.'

'Oh,' said Ruby thoughtfully. 'You see all sides, don't you?'

'If I didn't, I'd be really in trouble this time.'

'Yes,' Ruby agreed, and got off the bed. She drew her dressing-gown round her more tightly. It was a pink and white one, quilted, and rather short, so that her pyjama'd legs showed, and it just outlined the slim lines of her figure; she had very narrow hips, and there was really only a hint of shape at her breast. 'Would you like a whisky and water, or some tea?'

'A finger of neat whisky and then some tea would be wonderful,' said Dawlish, 'but oughtn't you—'

'If you weren't too preoccupied with other matters, you'd know that if I put out the light and went to sleep it would be most unfeminine, and whenever a female behaves with remark-able unfemininity, the police are likely to wonder why.' Ruby went to a corner, which was curtained off, and drew it back to show a small sink, two cupboards fastened to the wall, and a small gas cooker. She filled an aluminium kettle noisily, and then lit the gas; it popped.

'I think I ought to slip out and see what's happening now,' she said. 'Do you think you ought to hide again?'

'I'll be all right if you lock the door.'

'Yes, I suppose so.' She took the key out of the inside of the lock. 'When I went down before there was a lot of excitement, and the police wouldn't let anyone go down to the ground floor. I expect it will be easier now.' She turned the door-handle. Dawlish felt his breath coming faster, and stared fixedly at her as she opened the door boldly, and looked outside. A moment later, she turned back, smiling, and whispered: 'All clear up here.' She went out, pulling the door to with a snap and he heard her footsteps as she went down the shiny stairs.

The gas was hissing under the kettle.

Dawlish went across and helped himself to a little whisky. He drank slowly, savouring it. He could have swallowed a whole glassful, but that would do him no good. He stared at the bluish flame, then stepped to the window and peered out through the edge of the curtains. There were flashlights outside, and the beam of a searchlight, probably a motor-cycle headlamp. He could just detect the figures of several men moving about. He turned back, and looked bleakly at the door. The police were likely to keep watch closely on this house, and he had no real chance of getting out now; almost no hope of being back at Four Ways before dawn.

'No hope at all,' he told himself, savagely.

There was the one bright spot: Mrs Wattle's admission.

There was the puzzle about Ruby Ard's behaviour, too. It was remarkable that whenever he was particularly surprised by something she did, she gave an explanation, quite pat, even before he asked for it; as if she could read his thoughts. That was ludicrous, yet the notion entered his head. He finished the whisky, then swung round abruptly; this room might be worth searching.

He found and opened two handbags; they had oddments in them, but nothing which helped him. He found a writing-case, very neatly kept, with letters filed away; they included two letters from her sister, dated three months or so ago. Each letter told of her fears, and the strange men who were following her. There was a photograph of Marion, too, the same one as the newspapers had used; the girl looked no more than a child.

There was also a book of matches, obviously old, which advertised the Pack of Lies—like the liquor bills downstairs. The second appearance of the name of the pub was an odd coincidence, especially as it was miles away, and across the river.

Stacked in the foot of the wardrobe were newspapers which carried the story of Marion's disappearance, and also the discovery of her body; there was nothing new in any of this for him.

The kettle was singing and steam came wispily from the spout. Dawlish was still thirsty, and a little cold; but he turned the gas down, not wanting the kettle to boil until Ruby came back. He went to the door and listened, but heard nothing, although she must have been gone for ten minutes. He did not think that she had intended to be away for so long. He lit a cigarette, wondering whether it was wise; but the smoke would not get outside, the only danger would be if the police came to search again.

Why didn't Ruby return?

Was she caught up with the other tenants, aping their curiosity so as not to make herself noticeable? Or were the police questioning her? If they were, would she be able to lie to them effectively? She seemed calm and fully capable of doing whatever she wanted, but the police were used to dealing with much tougher people than Ruby Ard.

Dawlish finished the cigarette.

Why didn't she come back?

The kettle was boiling; either he had to make the tea, or stand the kettle off the ring. His mouth was tacky, and the whisky seemed to beckon him, but if an emergency came he must be absolutely clear-headed. He took a teapot down from the shelf in one of the cupboards, found a pale blue tin tea caddy, and made tea. Some milk was in a bottle, standing in the window to keep cool. He put all this and two cups and saucers on a tray, almost from force of habit; and then told himself what a crazy thing it was, if the police should come back with her. . . .

The game would be up then, anyhow.

He poured a cup of tea, and was drinking it when he heard voices of two people coming up the stairs; two women. There might be a policewoman with Ruby. Dawlish looked longingly at the bed, but decided that it would be a waste of time to try to hide there. He stepped behind the door, so that he couldn't be seen by anyone standing outside, and then saw that the tray was in full view of anyone in the doorway. He went across and picked up his cup, and put the tray in a corner. He heard a woman saying, 'Terrible,' and 'Isn't it awful?' and 'What a dreadful thing to happen,' but he gave no thought to that, or to Ruby's non-committal answers. Then the handle of the door turned, and she opened the door an inch, speaking clearly, and obviously making sure that he heard every word, 'I really must go and get some sleep now, I'll be no good at all in the morning.'

'You couldn't *sleep* after that, could you?'

'Fussy fool,' thought Dawlish, and pressed close against the wall as the door opened.

Ruby stepped inside, and closed and locked the door again, but this time she did not smile. She stood with her back to the door, the key in her hand, and it was impossible to guess the thoughts in her mind, or the reasons for her expression. But she put a new kind of apprehension into Dawlish.

She said: 'Don't try it with me, one scream would bring a dozen policemen running.'

He stood still, cup and saucer in hand, and said:

'I don't get it.'

'Mrs Wattle is lying downstairs with her head smashed in,' Ruby announced, with great precision. 'Apparently she was struck two very powerful blows, one on the forehead, and one on top of the head. She is dead. It is obvious to everyone that she saw the burglar, and that he killed her to stop her from identifying him.'

Dawlish did not move.

Ruby stood and stared, with accusation in her eyes.

He remembered the landlady's scream, when he had been in the passage, even remembered assuming that she had become hysterical. Instead, she had seen Hillman with weapon raised, about to strike and kill her.

No one else had seen Hillman doing that, though.

13

HIDING PLACE

Ruby was watching Dawlish intently, and he could see that her right hand, behind her back, was near the handle of the door, and the key. If he made a move to attack her, she could open it and scream. He stood very still, without moving; and then gradually began to smile. In an odd way, he felt like smiling; here he stood with the delicate cup and saucer in his hand, ready to sip tea like any old dame at a tea-party; and there was Ruby Ard, prepared to open that door and shout, yet watching him as if she still could not make up her mind what to think about him.

'So it's amusing,' she said.

'It isn't amusing if you're thinking of Mrs Wattle,' Dawlish said, 'but if you could take a photograph of the pair of us, it would raise a smile. They're determined to make sure that I get landed with murder, aren't they? Bertie Hillman has a mind that really works fast.'

'Tell me more,' invited Ruby.

Dawlish said, 'Open the door a crack, and make sure no one's coming up, will you?'

'There's a party of police on the roof, I heard someone say they'd soon be finished,' Ruby answered, 'and they're taking photographs and vacuum-cleaning the hall and the first flight of stairs. Everyone takes it for granted that you got away.'

'Yes. Thanks.'

Ruby opened the door, and there were only distant sounds, including the whirr of a vacuum cleaner. She closed the door and turned the key in the lock, then moved away. He had seldom seen a girl with cooler courage. For all she knew, he was the killer of two women, and for all she knew, he would attack her because she could identify him. But she had taken her stand; and now she moved to the corner table where Dawlish had put the tray, and began to pour out a cup of tea. That was when he noticed the beads of perspiration at her upper lip, and saw that the excitement had faded, and her cheeks were without colour.

She dropped into a chair.

The cup rattled on the saucer, because her hands began to shake.

'I hope I'm right about you,' she managed to say.

'I'm glad you're human,' Dawlish said dryly. 'I was beginning to wonder. You want a lot of sugar in that tea, you'll feel better then.' She let him put three heaped spoonfuls in, and then stirred it; she was steadier, and looked up at him with a smile that was only slightly tremulous. 'And you're right about me. Hillman killed her, of course.'

She gulped tea down.

'Ugh, that's sickly. Well, obviously if it wasn't you, it must have been Hillman.' She gulped again. 'But it won't be easy to prove, will it?' She finished the tea. 'May I have a cup without sugar now?'

'In a few minutes. It will be ten times more difficult than proving that I didn't kill your sister.'

'Did Hillman see you?'

'Yes. He caught me by surprise.'

'He must be very clever,' she remarked. She was silent for a moment, and then went on: 'You couldn't possibly prove that you'd been somewhere else, could you?'

'Not unless I'm back in my own house by half past four,' answered Dawlish. 'I came in a car the police will have examined by now, and they'll soon find out that I borrowed it from a neighbour. So even that's out.'

'What does it mean?'

'I can prove I didn't kill either your sister or this woman only one way, by finding out who did.'

She said: 'And I thought *I* had a problem!' She held out her cup, and he took it and poured out another cup of tea, added a little milk, and gave it to her. 'I heard them talking among themselves.'

'The police?'

'Yes. They've this search party on the roof, and they're having all the streets leading into this one cordoned off. They don't think you can have got out of the neighbourhood, and they think you're probably hiding in a garden, or else you've broken into another house. They're going to search outside until six o'clock, and if they haven't found you then, they're going to search every house in the terrace. The man from Scotland Yard was giving the orders.'

'So Penfold's here in person,' Dawlish said heavily. 'I take it that you're advising me not to try to escape until they've given up hope of finding me here?'

'And that will be a long time,' Ruby said. She sipped the hot, strong tea with obvious relish, and when she put her cup down, was smiling in an oddly amused way. 'It looks as if I shall have to sleep with a man who might have murdered my sister!'

'Ruby,' Dawlish said, and he had not used her Christian name before.

Her eyes smiled in a nice enough way.

'Yes, Pat?'

'If the police find out what you're doing, you'll be held as an accessory, and there's already the suspicion about the other murder.'

'I know.'

'I can tell you what you ought to do.'

'I know what I ought to do: I ought to open the door and shout police—it would do even if I threw this cup through the window, they'd come running in a posse. But I can't make myself do it, Patrick Dawlish! All the way up the stairs, after I heard what had happened, I told myself what I ought to do. Any sane person would turn you in. I actually *said* it to myself. And then I kept seeing your face and hearing your voice, the way it was this afternoon. I can't see you as a woman-killer, simply can't see you in the part. I told myself that when I opened the door I'd know in a moment if you were a murderer or not. I just don't believe you are.'

'That won't help you much in a court of law,' Dawlish said, softly. 'If they catch me here, they'll charge me, and they'll try to make it stick. They'll charge you as an accessory, too.'

'What's the matter, do you *want* me to turn you in?'

'If you raise your voice any more, it'll be done automatically,' Dawlish said, without looking away from her. 'I want to be absolutely sure you know what you're doing.'

'I know what I'm doing,' Ruby declared, chokily. She looked at the door, and he could imagine the temptation to jump up, open it and shout 'Police!' 'What I can't make out is whether I'm mad. Do you think the police will come and look in the room again?'

'They probably won't until they've finished the search outside,'

Dawlish guessed after a moment's thought, 'but I wouldn't be sure which way Penfold will jump. Do you know what the window ledges are like outside?'

'I don't understand you.'

'If they knock on the door, I'll have to get out of the window and hope that no one's watching from below,' Dawlish said. 'If it comes to a pinch I could hang from the window-sill, but not for long.'

Ruby looked angry and, when she spoke, sounded angry.

'Why are you making everything sound so difficult?'

'Ruby,' said Dawlish, very steadily, 'I want to stay here until tomorrow night. At about half past one, I want to get up and go and see Hillman. After that, I might be able to go to the police. Once I'm out of this room I won't come back, and you'll have nothing to fear then.'

'I see,' said Ruby, slowly. 'I suppose you're right. But what are we going to do now?'

'One of us ought to take a nap and the other keep awake,' Dawlish answered. 'Do you have any office to go to in the morning?'

'No.'

'Then it doesn't matter what time we're about. You sleep first, I'll call you about six.'

'Sleep,' she echoed, and it was almost a sneer.

'You'll sleep,' he assured her. 'You'll be surprised how well!' He took her cup and saucer and put them on the tray, pulled up a wicker armchair which was barely large enough for him but was the only one in the room, and sat down. She went across to the bed, and took off her dressing-gown; she was still as modestly attired as a schoolgirl, but her legs were seductively slim and beautiful as she slid them between the sheets.

She whispered.

'Good night.'

'Good night.'

She put out the light.

Was she awake? Dawlish wondered.

It was an hour since she had turned out the light; and for some time she had been restless, turning this way and that, punching her pillow often, but keeping very quiet. Now her breathing seemed steadier, and he thought she was asleep. He was cramped and uncomfortable, and wanted to get up and walk round the room; but if he did, he would bang into something, and disturb her.

There had been many other sounds.

The party from the roof; the party on the stairs, looking for clues; the distant noises of car engines; now and again, clear voices from the street and gardens; once, the ringing of an ambulance bell, which had come very near; the ambulance had come for the woman's body, of course. Dawlish could see that man's thin, sallow face in front of his eyes all the time; the dark, intelligent eyes of a man who had seen an opportunity and snatched it in the space of seconds. Hillman had heard Mrs Wattle make her confession, of course, and known that she could not be trusted; so he had killed her.

Would the police be fooled?

Penfold would believe the worst of Dawlish if he had half a chance, and Penfold was in charge.

But they'd be thorough; they would check on all details, and get to Hillman, sooner or later.

Wouldn't they?

Penfold was sitting at a small table in the living-room of Mrs Wattle's flat. Two plain-clothes men were with him, one taking notes, the other studying a pile of oddments which were on the sideboard with the mirror back. There were matchsticks, cigarette ends, little envelopes containing fluff, dust, grit, a dozen things which the vacuum cleaner had picked up. There was the piece of iron piping, bloodstained at one end, with strands of Mrs Wattle's dyed auburn hair sticking to it; to Penfold and the others it might have been mud. There were a few strands of grass, each in an envelope, some short hairs, and some coins.

The plain-clothes man, King, finished writing. He looked very tired as he turned to Penfold, and said:

'That's everything.'

'Sure?'

'Yes, sir.'

'How about the plaster casts on those big footprints we found in the flower-beds next door and next door to that?'

'They're done, and as soon as they're hard, they'll be taken along to the lab.'

'Right,' said Penfold. He rubbed his eyes, which looked so red that they might have been inflamed. 'Now, what've we got? Hillman says it was Dawlish, said he recognised him from a photograph in the *Globe*. These footprints are size twelve, Dawlish's size. Can't find any of Dawlish's finger-prints here, but there are some prints made by cotton gloves, the kind he'd be likely to wear.' Penfold stifled a yawn. 'When the devil are Haslemere going to call back?' He glowered at the telephone, and as if to glower in turn, it rang. He snatched up the receiver. 'Penfold here, at Harven Street,' he announced. 'Eh? . . . Yes, what did they say?' He listened, and suddenly began to smile; smiling, he looked less tired. 'Yes, that's fine,' he said. 'Thanks.' He put down the receiver, and glanced across at King, who waited with calmness that amounted almost to indifference.

'Dawlish isn't in his house. He got out through a back window, and used a neighbouring farmer's car—an Austin, black, registration number 12PR 54.'

'That's the number of the one we found in the next street,' King said; his interest flared.

'That's right,' agreed Penfold, and sounded almost smug. 'That's got Dawlish so tightly he'll never get clear once we get our hands on him.'

'He can't be far away.'

'He's a clever man, and he'll use all the wits God gave him to get away with this.'

'Clever,' echoed King, and frowned a little; and then stifled a yawn. 'I'd never met Dawlish before, only heard of him,' he said. 'He was a kind of fabulous figure one read and heard about. I've often studied his cases, though, and he's clever all right.'

'What are you driving at?' asked Penfold.

'If he's so clever, why's he done all this? Leaving Marion Ard's body in that storeroom to begin with—'

'He didn't have a chance to move it, and he didn't think anyone would find it in a locked room until he got back. He could have buried everything, trunk and all, in those grounds of his, probably wouldn't have found it for years.' Penfold was almost aggressive.

'Then why didn't he bury it, and make sure there wasn't a smell?' demanded King.

Penfold said: 'He hadn't enough time.'

'That wasn't so smart, then. And was it clever to come here and kill the old woman? Frightened the wits out of her, perhaps, if he thought she was lying, but to kill her—I don't think it's very clever.'

'All right,' said Penfold, sharply, 'so he's acting out of character. A desperate man often does, I don't have to tell you that.

The man must have a mad streak, and once the Ard girl started to threaten his home life, it came out.'

King didn't speak.

'Not convinced?' asked Penfold.

'Well,' answered King, 'it's not a case of being convinced, is it? It's a case of acquiring the evidence, and there's a lot of it. But I'd like to know what drove Dawlish to cut loose like this. It's all very well for a chap to have a girl on the side, but all the reports I've heard say that he's happily married.'

Penfold snorted. 'I didn't know you were a romantic.'

'Just looking at reported facts,' said King, placidly. 'Funny thing, I did once meet his wife. Charming woman, too. I could quite understand it when everyone said that Dawlish was a one-woman man. She's the one I feel most sorry for. Any idea where she is?'

'Yes,' answered Penfold. 'She caught tonight's plane from Cairo, and will be in London in the morning. The newspaperman Nimmo telephoned his office, and they rang me. Mrs Dawlish saw an English newspaper story about finding the body in the trunk, and after that she moved as fast as Dawlish.'

King said musingly: 'If Dawlish did it, think his wife knew?'

'You can never tell with this so-called upper class,' said Penfold. 'A man can have a dozen mistresses, but if there's trouble, his wife stands by him. We'll soon find out. I gave the *Globe* tonight's story an hour ahead of the other newspapers, but every front page will carry a picture of Dawlish in the morning.'

King nodded.

'Now let's see what's doing outside,' Penfold said briskly, and stood up. 'We've a cordon as tight as wire netting round the neighbourhood. Dawlish can't possibly have got through it.'

King's expression seemed to say: 'Can't he?'

14

FELICITY COMES HOME

Felicity stepped off the plane at London Airport, and was startled when half a dozen newspaper cameramen stepped in front of her. Lights flashed and cameras clicked, and a man at the side said:

'Can we say you've every faith in your husband, Mrs Dawlish?'

Felicity fought back irritation at the onslaught; it would serve no purpose if she annoyed the Press. She even made herself smile.

'You can say I've every confidence in the world.'

'Did you know Miss Marion Ard?' a man called out.

'I can't say anything about the case itself,' Felicity answered, and then realised that the response might be construed into a refusal to answer the question. Well; it couldn't be helped.

'Can we say you're an ideally happy couple?' another man called.

'I don't know that I want you to say it, but I've been happily married for fifteen years,' said Felicity. 'Now you really must excuse me.'

They stood aside.

She looked towards the airport enclosure, for some sign

of Pat; there was none. There were dozens of people, probably nearly a hundred; but she would have picked Pat out at a glance, because of his size. She hurried towards the entrance to the customs bay, and there was still no sign of Pat, but she caught sight of an old friend of Pat's, and of hers. Ted Beresford was also a big man, if not so tall as Dawlish, and running to fat. He waved. Felicity had no chance to speak to him, but went into the customs bay more worried even than before. Beresford and his wife Joan had been in the South of France, and were supposed to be staying there most of the year.

Ted had come back to help, of course, but—why not Tim? And why not Pat himself? Was it possible that he was under arrest?

Felicity was aware of the customs officers looking at her curiously. They were perfunctory in their questions, and the whole procedure did not take more than five minutes. She hurried out, tall and long-legged and slim; more cameras clicked. She wanted to talk to Ted above everything else, and saw him fifty yards away, looking rather untidy, dark hair rumpled, big hands gesticulating in some kind of protest. He was talking to a spindly, rather inadequate kind of man.

Two others, one big, dressed in a dark blue suit which seemed too small for him, and with a boyish face, came up to her. She had seen this man before somewhere, and was quite sure that he was from Scotland Yard.

'Good morning, Mrs Dawlish.'

'Good morning.'

'I am Detective-Inspector Penfold, of New Scotland Yard.'

Felicity felt almost sure that he was going to add that Pat was under arrest, but she did not prompt him. He looked very tired, and his eyes were so red that she felt almost sorry for him. She saw Ted, still arguing; and then another man whom she did not recognise joined Ted; this man was of medium height, and dressed immaculately.

Pat would have been here if he could possibly have made it.

'I wonder if you will be good enough to come along to Scotland Yard and answer a few questions, Mrs Dawlish,' Penfold asked.

She kept her fears to herself.

'At once?'

'Yes, please.'

'Why is it necessary?'

'We are investigating a murder case, Mrs Dawlish; surely you are aware of that.'

'There is nothing I can say to help you.'

'You can't be sure,' Penfold said. Obviously he was fighting to keep civil, but there was an edge in his voice. Certainly he had the look of a man who had been up all night; Felicity had often seen Pat like this, after he had been out on some wild venture. Usually, he had gone to look for trouble; she had always known that the spirit of St George was in him, and that it would never really die. The bitter thing was that this time he had tried so hard to stifle it.

'This way, Mrs Dawlish, please,' Penfold added.

Felicity hesitated.

She wondered what Pat would do in circumstances like these; whether he would accede meekly to the request, or flatly refuse. The important thing was to do whatever would help most, and it would not help to exasperate the police any more than it would help to make the newspapermen angry. She had better go. She saw that the crowd about them was much thicker now—hundreds of people had gathered down here. When she went out with Penfold, a crowd had gathered there, too, and more cameras were aimed at her. A police car was waiting, and Penfold put a hand on her arm, holding her tightly, as if to hustle her towards the car.

'Take your hand away, please,' Felicity said sharply.

Penfold snatched his hand away.

There was a sea of faces, but the only one she wanted wasn't there. 'Pat, where *are* you? And why are these people gaping, as if at some new sensation?' The murder had been discovered four days ago; surely there had been fresh sensations to take the public mind off Pat.

A man called: 'Inspector, just a moment.'

They were at the side of the car. Penfold ignored the call, and opened the door; he gave the impression that he would gladly push her in.

The man called: 'Inspector, if you refuse to allow me to talk with my client, I shall make the strongest possible protest to the Home Office.'

His client?

Penfold stopped and turned round with manifest reluctance. The rather innocuous-looking man who had been talking to Ted Beresford was there, and Ted himself was at the front of the crowd, with the slim, dark-clad, immaculate man. Ted waved again, and smiled, but it was a peculiar kind of smile, with none of the brightness and the warmth natural to Ted. He was scared. He pushed his way through to the front, and hurried towards Felicity, while the smaller man looked at her, and Penfold muttered under his breath.

'Hallo, Ted,' Felicity said.

They gripped hands. 'Hallo, Fel.'

'Ted, what's happened? Have they arrested Pat?'

Ted Beresford said, with unexpected bitterness: 'I wish to God they'd arrested him last night.'

Felicity felt the crushing pressure of his hands, and saw the distress in his eyes. She did not even begin to understand, but was more frightened than she had ever been. There was some disastrous news, which even Ted hated to tell her.

Was Pat *dead*?

'Ted, what is it? Don't just stand there gaping, tell me what's happened.'

'Mrs Dawlish'—the immaculate young man began, with a quick, rather pleasant, smile, 'I think we had better find a quieter spot where we can talk.'

'There is a warrant out for the arrest of your husband on a charge of murdering a Mrs Wattle, at a house in Kensington, last night,' Penfold put in, and he seemed to take pleasure in making the announcement. 'He is avoiding arrest.'

First, Felicity felt a sense of relief, but that soon left her. The detective's words made no more sense than Ted's embarrassment. A warrant for the arrest for a woman's murder *last* night?

She looked at Ted. His eyes confirmed what Penfold had said, and Felicity understood his manner now, knew that he felt as if there was no hope at all; as if he *believed* that Pat had committed this murder. Ted, of all people; Pat's closest and oldest friend—why, it was crazy.

'Don't talk nonsense,' she said roundly to Penfold. 'My husband didn't murder anyone.'

'Mrs Dawlish—'

'Mrs Dawlish,' interrupted the immaculate young man, 'I must advise you to make no statement of any kind to the police until we have had an opportunity to discuss this matter.' He was crisp and businesslike.

'I want to talk to Mrs Dawlish at the Yard,' Penfold insisted grimly. 'She will have plenty of time to consult you afterwards,

Mr Osborne. Mrs Dawlish, the quicker we get to Scotland Yard the quicker you will be free.'

'We'll come to the Yard and wait there for you,' Ted said. He was gripping the smaller man's arm, obviously advising him not to rile Penfold any further.

He looked so miserable and unhappy.

Ted believed that Pat . . .

'I don't know what all this is about,' Felicity said in a very clear voice, 'but I do know that this is ludicrous. If Pat is hiding from the police, it's because he knows he'll find out the truth a long time before they will.'

She heard Penfold take in a hissing breath.

Someone at the back of the crowd laughed, and someone else called out:

'That's the spirit!'

Two or three people raised a little cheer.

Felicity stepped into the police car, and Penfold climbed in and sat by her side, looking straight ahead, and edging away so that he did not press against her. There was a crowd in front of the car, which uniformed police moved on. They moved slowly at first, then with gathering speed, and two cars came after them. Felicity stripped off one glove, opened her handbag, and took out cigarettes; she seldom smoked, but always carried a few cigarettes; she needed one now.

She blew smoke straight in front of her, and stared at the back of the police driver's head.

'What is this nonsense?' she asked, curtly.

'Mrs Dawlish, I've been up all night, and was up most of the night before,' Penfold said. 'I'm sorry if I've been inconsiderate.'

Felicity looked at him, her eyes still clear and cold.

'Will you please tell me what has happened?'

'Last night your husband went to see the woman where

Marion Ard lived, although he had been asked not to leave his home without advising us,' Penfold explained. 'He saw her, and killed her.'

'I don't believe it.'

'He was seen there, Mrs Dawlish.'

There was coldness at her heart, but she repeated:

'I don't believe it.'

'Mrs Dawlish, I don't expect you to believe the worst of your husband, and I'm sorry about your personal distress, but I'm a policeman, and I've a job to do. Mr Dawlish and Mr Jeremy made it extremely difficult for me to do it, and Mr Beresford isn't exactly co-operating. Mr Osborne, the solicitor we just saw, has taken an obstructive attitude, too. I want to talk to you as a witness, not as a suspect, and I cannot allow a witness to be prejudiced by any arguments.'

He was talking too much; probably he really hated this; or else he was so tired that he couldn't control his words properly.

'Whether or not he committed these crimes, a warrant is out for his arrest, and the quicker we have him in custody the better it will be for you and for him, Mrs Dawlish. And that's what I want to say to you. Do you know where he is likely to be hiding?'

Felicity knew of a dozen places.

'No,' she answered.

'Mrs Dawlish, no good will come from evasions,' Penfold said heavily. 'Your own and your husband's best interests will only be served if he gives himself up quickly. The longer he remains at large, the more it will look like an admission of guilt. If you know where we can find your husband, we must be told where it is. That is the important thing at the moment.'

'I haven't the faintest idea,' Felicity insisted.

'Very well,' said Penfold, and was silent for a few moments. Then he went on as if weary almost beyond words: 'We may as well start on the other matters, Mrs Dawlish.' He turned to look at her, and as he did so a voice sounded over the air, coming from a radio loudspeaker next to the driver. Felicity heard Penfold's name called, and then she heard the speaker say 'Dawlish'.

'. . . Dawlish has been reported seen near the London Docks area,' the man announced, and Penfold's tired eyes glinted, as if with satisfaction.

Felicity thought desperately: 'They mustn't catch him.'

15

FEAR

There were detectives. Penfold, King, others whose names she did not know. There were men with big faces, fat faces, thin faces, hungry faces; and they all asked Felicity questions, so politely and yet so insistently; they asked her the same questions too, and she knew quite well what they were trying to do: they wanted her to contradict herself, so that some answer she gave would make the situation even worse for Pat.

She had hardly slept on the aircraft.

She was pale, her voice was low-pitched and getting huskier.

She hated all the faces and hated all the questions; about Pat and this Marion Ard, this girl she had seen only once, with the great limpid eyes, standing in front of Pat, snatching off her worthless jewellery, thrusting it forward in her cupped hands, as payment for the help which Pat had not wanted to give.

'How long had your husband known Miss Ard, Mrs Dawlish?'

'He didn't know her, except for those few hours.'

'But at least two independent witnesses have said that they saw Mr Dawlish and Miss Ard together a month or more before May 30th.'

'I can't help that.'

'When Miss Ard came to your house, Mrs Dawlish, did she appear to know your husband?'

'No.'

'We know how distressing such questions are, Mrs Dawlish, but had you any reason to believe that your husband was interested in another woman?'

'No.'

'Surely there would be *some* indication, Mrs Dawlish?'

A cup of tea.

Questions.

Fat, thin, broad, long, handsome, ugly faces.

A cigarette.

Hard, soft, rounded, Cockney, Oxford voices.

A cup of tea.

A cigarette.

'Thank you very much for your patience, Mrs Dawlish,' Penfold said. It looked as if his eyelids would refuse to stay open another second; as if the moment Felicity's back was turned he would drop into a chair and fall asleep. 'If you have any kind of communication from your husband, it will be in your best interests to inform us at once.' That was like a record.

Felicity did not even speak.

Then she was with Ted on one side, big kindly, ugly, paunchy Ted, who walked slowly and stiffly because of an artificial leg. Years ago, centuries ago, when he and Pat had served in MI5 together Ted had lost a leg; he and Pat had been lucky then not to lose their lives. The danger that Pat had faced in his lifetime had been fantastic; no man had risked so much, no man had been more heedless of danger.

He had been wounded, but never closer to death, never in greater peril, than he was now.

She had been in England for four hours, and was sure of that already.

She was walking through the corridors of the Yard, where once he had thought that he might walk as Assistant Commissioner for Crime. What did these fools think they were doing, suspecting Pat of murder? It was crazy, it was criminal. He *caught* murderers. He had helped the Yard a dozen, a hundred, times to catch killers, because he had always hated murderers. He always rejected the argument that blackmail and dope-peddling were the worst crimes; the act of murder, the act of killing for gain or revenge, had seemed to him the greatest crime of all.

He had been bitterly opposed to the abolition of the death penalty.

'We're not ready for it yet,' he had said. 'If a man kills another deliberately and wilfully, he should be killed in turn.'

He was wanted for *two* murders.

There was this old woman, this landlady. Why *her*?

Last night, when Felicity had been in the air, anxious and rest-less, but sure that she would be seeing Pat in the morning, this woman had been battered to death. The police seemed so posi-tive that Pat had killed her; what was worse, there was Ted's glumness, and there was the irritating firmness of the footsteps of the solicitor, Osborne.

At last they were in Ted's big old Bentley, driving out of the Yard.

'Joan didn't come,' Ted said. 'I told her I'd send for her if it would help.'

'How is she?' Felicity asked, mechanically, and did not hear his answer. 'Ted, what's the matter with you? Why are you acting as if Pat did this thing?'

'Fel, it's the last thing I'd dream of believing!'

'Well, you're behaving as if you think he did it.'

Osborne interrupted, with a wave of his hand. He was such a complete young man, his collar and tie were just right, his suit was beautifully cut, his features were good, his complexion had been won on playing fields, he had bright grey eyes and an alert look, his hands were strong and yet not large; they were beautifully kept, and he had a well-modulated voice and a friendly smile, yet not one that was overdone.

'Mrs Dawlish, I can assure you that Mr Beresford has made it abundantly clear that he does not think there is the slightest possibility that your husband is guilty. However, as a lawyer, I want to help in every way I can, and it will not be helpful if I mislead you. The police believe that the evidence against your husband, for the murder of the woman Wattle, in Harven Street, is very great indeed. This is not one of the cases where the police release half a story, and leave us guessing at what they are keeping up their sleeve. It is obvious that they do not think there is any need to keep anything at all up their sleeve. And, speaking as a lawyer, without sentiment or emotion, I must say that I can understand their point of view.'

'I want to know exactly what happened last night,' Felicity said. Osborne told her.

Ted stared moodily out of the window at traffic lights and blocks, turned into the mews where he and his wife had a London flat which had once been the common property of Dawlish, Beresford and several other friends; it was the place where Dawlish and Felicity had spent their honeymoon. Osborne was still outlining the police case, making it obvious that the Yard had good grounds for suspecting Pat.

'The case is so strong I'd mistrust it on those grounds alone,' Osborne said. 'But until we test its strength we won't find out its weakness.'

Pat often said something like that.

'I'll nip along to the shop at the corner and get some oddments,' said Ted. 'Better make a cuppa here, rather than go where crowds can gawp at us. Bit of luck that no one's guessed where you'll be.'

Felicity saw a man standing at a garage opposite the front door of the mews flat, and was sure that it was a policeman. She saw a car stop at the end of the mews; another policeman would probably be in that. She knew that Penfold was positive that Pat would try to get in touch with her, and so he would watch her wherever she went.

There was Ted, with his understandable gloom.

'. . . and unless we see the situation at its worst, we cannot hope to be able to help your husband,' Osborne was saying. They were in the big room of the flat, drawing-room at one end, with a small dining alcove. Joan Beresford had not used dust sheets anywhere, and had not cleared away the ornaments and oddments. On the small piano were several photographs, one of Pat and Ted together, in uniform, taken fifteen years ago; they looked like big boys.

'. . . and what we have to establish beyond all doubt, Mrs Dawlish, is the truth or otherwise of your husband's assertion that he did not know Marion Ard until May 31st. If it can be established beyond all doubt that he did know her, and the police believe that it can, then—'

'Mr Osborne,' Felicity said, 'my husband did not know that girl, and the police are wrong. Pat saw her for the first time when she visited us at Four Ways. He had talked to her twice on the telephone, each time asking her not to expect help from him.'

'Mrs Dawlish,' Osborne retorted, with that little prim smile, 'I can understand your feelings on this matter, but I am not acting on behalf of the police, and everything you tell me will be in the strictest confidence. I believe absolutely in your husband's innocence, and my only concern is to prove it. That isn't because of a particular sense of justice, but because Marion Ard was my client. She told me about these fears, and I made light of them, believing she was neurasthenic. Her murder was not only a great shock to me, but a severe jolt to my conscience. I threw away my chance to help her; I mean to take every chance I can to avenge her.'

He spoke very quietly and impressively, and Felicity felt the strength of his determination.

'I know enough of your husband's reputation not to believe he killed Marion, and therefore he is being framed.' Osborne spread his hands. 'By finding who is doing that, we shall find the murderer. Do you see my point?'

'Of course,' said Felicity.

'Then I hope you will allow me to get under the skin of the police case as it were, without thinking I share their opinion. In my considered view, had they felt confidence in the evidence available, they would have arrested Mr Dawlish for the Marion Ard crime immediately he reached England. There were, however, obvious doubts. The first: why did he leave the body in the trunk, where obviously it might be found? One answer might be that he was extremely pushed for time and that as the trunk was a comparatively airtight container, he might reasonably hope that the body would not decompose or become offensive. The police might also consider that your husband assumed that he would have ample time to dispose of the body on his return. Had he buried it in the garden immediately, his gardener might have seen evidence of recent digging, and investigated. However, in that regard we are dealing with surmise, and my task is to try to find out the facts. The fact immediately relevant

125

is that Mrs Wattle was murdered at about one o'clock this morning, when you were flying over the Mediterranean. You may have faith in your husband, you may be able to give him a kind of alibi for the first murder. You cannot give evidence to say that Mr Dawlish did not kill Mrs Wattle.'

The logic was hateful.

'And the police know that as well as I do.' Osborne went on.

Felicity nodded.

Osborne's smile became positively bright.

'I can understand your feelings, Mrs Dawlish, and of course if you desire it I will stop this assessment, but as Mr Jeremy knew, before he went away, I have been studying the case closely for some time. Finding the truth has become an obsession with me. Both I and Mr Jeremy were given to understand by Mrs Wattle that your husband had been to the house in Harven Street to see Miss Marion Ard and, in fact, had slept there on at least two occasions, earlier this year. Mr Jeremy did not believe this. However, I have had Mrs Wattle questioned by three different individuals, and they were all told the same thing: that your husband did in fact visit the young woman at the Harven Street house on a number of occasions, and stay the night.'

Felicity closed her eyes, feeling as if an unbearable weight were pressing on her forehead.

At least once a month, Pat stayed in town; 'at his club'.

Sometimes twice a month.

No wonder Ted had been so gloomy and dispirited, and Penfold was so absolutely sure of himself.

Osborne was saying:

'Of course, the police have that evidence up their sleeve. Mrs Wattle has made several visits to Scotland Yard and doubtless signed a detailed statement. And as far as I can trace, *only* Mrs

Wattle would be in a position to testify that your husband visited Miss Ard at Harven Street. So the one witness who mattered was Mrs Wattle. If, through her testimony, the police could satisfy a jury that Miss Ard was your husband's mistress . . .'

Why could a single word stab like a sword?

'. . . then the prosecution would obviously have a strong case. It could be argued that Miss Ard went to see him at Four Ways, that she endeavoured to disrupt his home life, and that in consequence he killed her, and later killed Mrs Wattle, so as to silence a witness. Now *there* is the whole issue as the police see it, Mrs Dawlish. Was this young woman threatening to break up your home life? If so, there is the strongest possible motive for murder—one strong enough to turn even a man with your husband's reputation into a murderer.'

'I see,' Felicity said; and it was hard to get the words out. 'What—what can you do?'

'I admit that I sometimes feel that I am powerless, Mrs Dawlish, and that the circumstances are too much for me. But I do not think it is really hopeless. If your husband did not kill Marion, someone did. Presumably it was a person who knew her, or else one who has black hatred for your husband. So I want to know if you can name anyone who might want your husband dead. I also want to know if Marion told your husband anything that she did not tell me, as her solicitor.'

That was the moment when Ted arrived, holding a large brown paper bag full of groceries.

'I've told him the answer to the first question is no,' he interrupted. 'I don't know whether Marion said anything to Pat about guessing who was frightening her?'

'If she did he didn't tell me,' answered Felicity. 'Oh, what a ghastly situation.'

Ted said: 'I know. Hell. Hate the whole business.' He was

mumbling short sentences, and had never been more miserable. 'But facts speak for themselves. They—'

Felicity almost screamed: 'Pat didn't kill that Ard girl!'

'The police aren't going to charge him with that,' Ted muttered.

'I'm afraid that is true,' said Osborne.

'Fel, I've got to say this,' Ted Beresford went on heavily. 'Tim dug deep, and obviously hated what he found out. It's possible that he's gone off so that he can't be questioned about what he did discover. I mean, this association between Pat and Marion Ard. The Wattle woman was hellish sure. The basic fact is that Pat's in a hell of a mess,' Ted went on, rumbling. 'Just telephoned a chap I know at the *Daily Globe*. There was a false alarm at Wapping this morning. They haven't got Pat yet, but they're bound to, sooner or later.'

'Ted, what's the matter with you? Pat's never failed, has he? He's trying to find the real murderer, and—'

Ted said: 'I've never felt so badly. Osborne may be right, and someone with an old grudge is framing Pat. If he is, he's a genius. Look at the facts. Tim's out of England, as if avoiding the need to tell the police the truth. This old landlady's dead. The evidence that Pat was often at her house is overwhelming.'

Felicity said in shocked dismay: 'Don't you believe in Pat?'

'Of course I do, but—' Ted grunted and rumbled.

'Mr Osborne is right. Pat would look for the weakness in the police case, too,' Felicity went on, tensely. 'What about this man Hillman, who says he saw Pat, and tried to stop Pat from killing the old woman? Isn't Hillman a possible murderer?'

'First thing I said to Osborne this morning,' Ted told her.

'I'm putting private detectives on to Hillman at once,' Osborne said, 'but he was unconscious when the police found him, apparently. His nose was broken, too. According to the newspapers, he says that your husband hit him and left him for dead.'

'You know how Pat could punch when he was roused,' Ted put in. 'Broke a chap's nose once before. The police accept Hillman's story, not much doubt about that.'

'But Pat wouldn't kill a defenceless old woman!'

Ted didn't answer.

'Ted, what's the matter with you?' Felicity demanded. 'What's in your mind?'

'Fel,' said Ted, with awful distress, 'supposing Marion Ard's death was an accident. Supposing she—'

'*He didn't kill her!* And this Wattle woman's death wasn't an accident!'

'What Mr Beresford fears is that Mr Dawlish may be mentally ill,' Osborne interpolated. 'If we could find and talk to him, we would be able to find out. Have you any idea where he is, Mrs Dawlish?'

16

RUBY

'She's gone,' Ruby Ard answered. 'It'll be all right, I'll keep the door ajar.'

Dawlish said: 'Fine, thanks.'

They were standing near the door of Ruby's room, about half past eight on the morning after the murder. He had dozed and she had slept solidly for four hours, but they had been awake for half an hour, and Ruby had made tea, and then gone across and had a bath. She had told Dawlish that the neighbour across the landing left every morning at half past eight, to go to her office in the city; she might be late this morning but was usually a stickler for punctuality, fearing that her job might vanish if she didn't arrive on time.

She went hurrying, clattering on the stairs.

Ruby smiled; she looked as if she had slept quite well.

'It must be twenty-five minutes to nine, she's late. You can't be seen from the landing below, but I shouldn't dawdle in the bath, if I were you.'

'Bath' was a euphemism.

She was very good, very natural, almost sisterly. Dawlish

thought of the word as he opened the door, listened and heard the neighbour's fading footsteps, and then stepped on to the landing. The shabby walls, the yellow linoleum and the white-painted doors seemed to be all eyes. He opened the door of the bathroom, which had been temporarily repaired, and stepped in, then turned the key in the lock.

If the police did come up to look at the roof again, or examine the bathroom window, he wouldn't have a chance.

No one came.

The door of Ruby's room was closed, but not locked. Dawlish opened it, and slipped inside swiftly, his heart beating faster simply from the thought of being spotted.

Ruby was in the window, drawing a slip over her head. Her back was towards him, and one curtain was drawn so that she could not be seen from the outside, so she was like a silhouette. She wore a fragile-looking brassière and a pair of short, plain white knickers; no belt, no stockings. Her long slim legs were quite beautiful, and her waist looked small enough for him to span with both hands.

She wriggled until the slip was in position, and then turned to face him, quite unconcernedly.

'You ought to knock when you enter a lady's bedroom.'

'Sorry.'

'Fool,' she said, and laughed. 'You look almost shocked. And how many thousands of women have you seen in the nearly nude on a beach?'

'Dozens,' he said. 'Or thousands. But then I'm expecting it, and am on my guard.'

'Aren't you on your guard, now?'

'I'm getting there.'

She laughed again. 'Throw me over those stockings, will you?'

He looked round, found the flesh-coloured gossamer nylons and handed them to her. She was graceful in whatever she did;

even as she sat on a chair facing the window and put on her stockings. He could see her flawless shoulders, the narrow straps of bra and slip; and also her feet, where she rested them on the window-ledge. 'I hope you're not a big breakfast eater. I only have toast, marmalade and coffee, and there isn't much bread.'

'Seldom eat breakfast at all,' declared Dawlish.

'Liar. Did I tell you that I've an eleven o'clock appointment?'

'No.'

'I haven't told you much about myself at all, have I?' asked Ruby, and rolled her stockings at the top, then stood up. 'I earn a reasonable living selling books, I'm a representative of a publisher who specialises in needlework publications. I've an appointment at eleven, another at twelve, and one this afternoon, but I usually come home for lunch, so you won't be deprived of my company all day.'

'Bring back a nice big lunch,' begged Dawlish.

Then they heard footsteps, and Ruby looked as alarmed as he. He whispered: 'They've come to check across the landing,' and prayed that he was right. Three men went into the other flat, and were there for five minutes.

'They'll check here when you've gone,' Dawlish whispered.

'What will you do?'

'They've already checked your neighbour's room,' Dawlish answered.

'Well, you're experienced,' Ruby said.

She left a little after ten o'clock, dressed in a demure black and white check cotton suit. She had long, slim hands and slim, rather long, feet. She blew a kiss from the door as she went out, and Dawlish went across and shot the bolt; but he knew that he must not keep it shut for long.

The police would allow time to make sure that she did not come back unexpectedly, that was all. Dawlish judged that he had twenty minutes at most. He began to search this room; drawers in the dressing-chest, wardrobe, writing-case again, suitcases, clothes, even inside the radio. He found nothing that helped to explain why Ruby was taking such risks for him.

There was the Pack of Lies book of matches.

There were some notes in Spanish, too, and a photograph of a man and woman taken against the background of an unmistakably Spanish villa; the Ard parents. Marion the mother's girl, Ruby the father's. . . .

There was a photograph of Marion Ard in one of the suitcases, too. Dawlish imagined that it had been on show last night, that some time, when he had dozed off, Ruby had put it away. Dawlish studied it. They were alike and yet totally unlike. He wondered how well they had really got on, how well they had known each other. Then he put the photographs aside, and finished his search, as sure as he could be that nothing here would help him.

He had heard no sound of men approaching.

Dawlish left everything as he had found it, drew the bolt, turned the key and peered outside. He saw and heard nothing of the police. He stepped on to the landing, locked the door again and then tip-toed to the flat opposite. There was no key in the lock, but it was a simple kind, as easy as Ma Wattle's.

He began to force it.

Then he heard heavy footsteps in the hall.

His hand stiffened for a moment, and his hand became clumsy. There were two or three men. One spoke, but Dawlish did not hear the words. He had left this too late.

He began to work again, clenching his teeth, in a kind of frenzy. The men started up that first flight; they would be here in less than half a minute. If they were only going to search Ruby's room he would be safe enough in the bathroom, but if they tried the handle and found it locked they would wonder who was there. He groped blindly with the skeleton key. It caught, and slipped. The men were on the first landing. He had made a deadly mistake in searching the flat first, and should have come straight here. He fought to keep his hand steady, and the metal caught the lock again and held.

He turned it.

The click was so loud that he thought it must be heard by one of the oncoming men, who were near the second landing by now. He opened the door, stepped inside and closed the door so cautiously that he did not hear it click at all, which seemed a miracle, for the men were already on this narrow flight of stairs.

Would they come here again?

He heard them talking. A man laughed on a muted note. Then he heard the other door being opened, perhaps with a master key. The door creaked slightly when it was opened wide. He heard the men clump in; they would be cramped in that small space.

He sat on the bed in the punctual woman's flat, sweating for fear that he had left some clue that he had been in Ruby's room. He had not shaved. He had all his clothes on. He had washed up the breakfast things. He had checked that there was no grass or dirt off his shoes. He had tried to make sure that he had left no finger-prints, but it was almost impossible to be absolutely sure about everything like that. If he had overlooked one little thing, then they would be waiting for Ruby when she came home.

Ten minutes later, the men closed the door, and went downstairs.

Ruby was back at ten to one, for lunch. She brought morning newspapers. Dawlish's photograph was on all the front pages, but the reports said very little that he did not know.

Ruby, in a hurry, had little to say. Dawlish told her about the visitation, and she smiled congratulations. She was away again at half past two, and he decided that he could risk a sleep on the bed; the police had shown no further interest, there was no reason at all for them to suspect that he was in the house.

He was sleeping when the sound came at the door. He slept, as he had a thousand times before, so lightly that he was wide awake on the instant. The sound came again, of a key in the lock. He was lying on the bed, shoes off, collar undone, coat hanging over a chairback; otherwise he was dressed. He was poised to spring, for he could not be sure who this was; the police might have a key, or a master key. The door opened.

'It's me,' whispered Ruby.

She stepped in swiftly, and closed the door. She had a shopping bag in one hand and evening newspapers in the other. She stopped after closing the door and looked at him with her head a little on one side. She wasn't much more than twenty-five, and that dark hair, drawn back from her forehead, was a wonderful frame for her face, her clear unblemished complexion, and her dark blue eyes. She had changed while out, and wore a closely knitted jumper and skirt, of bright red; the red was almost too vivid, and yet it suited her.

'Had a good sleep?'

'Yes, thanks.'

'You look better.'

'I'd look better still if I had a razor.'

'I bought a blade for mine, and a tube of shaving cream,' Ruby told him, 'so you'll be able to clean up for dinner. Ham and salad, if you can stand it again.'

'Wonderful!'

'Liar,' she said. 'I nearly bought a huge steak, but somehow

I felt conspicuous wherever I went, and decided not to take a chance. It's very good ham.' She went to the corner and began to unpack, then turned and tossed the evening paper at him. 'She's very nice, isn't she?'

Dawlish didn't ask 'Who?'

Felicity's face peered up at him; a close-up taken some time ago and showing her at her best, and another taken at the airport that morning, surrounded by people. She looked good; she looked perfectly poised, too.

The headline read:

I LOVE MY HUSBAND AND HAVE EVERY FAITH IN HIM. . . .
Mrs Dawlish

'Touching,' Ruby said, and Dawlish glanced up, because it seemed as if there was a touch of tartness in her voice; but she was smiling. 'They haven't found you yet, and they think it's possible that you got out of the country. They've discovered that your friend Timothy Jeremy is somewhere in France.'

'Sure?' asked Dawlish, and scanned the story tensely. He saw nothing about that.

'It's on the back page,' Ruby told him. 'Apparently he travelled third class on a packed cross-Channel steamer on Friday, but one of the crew served in his battalion during the war, and recognised him.'

Dawlish said: 'I see,' and turned over and confirmed what she had said. He was sitting on the side of the bed, and looking enormous; his fair stubble, hardly touched with grey, caught the light.

'And you broke Hillman's nose,' announced Ruby.

'One good thing,' said Dawlish, but he was frowning. 'That I can't understand.'

'You're a very muscular man.'

'I mean, Tim going off. I could understand him lying low for a bit, and trying to contact me, but why should he rush to get out of the country?'

'He must have believed the worst. Pat . . .'

'Yes?'

'I shouldn't think there are many people who don't. I've heard dozens of people talking about it this afternoon, and everyone takes if for granted that you're guilty.'

'Ah,' said Dawlish, very softly. 'And you?'

'I'm feeding you, aren't I?'

'I'm not yet sure that I know why.'

She turned and looked at him, stepped towards him, put her hands on either side of his face, squeezed, and then kissed his lips lightly.

'Let's say it's love at first sight.'

'Let's not,' said Dawlish, very slowly. 'I couldn't stand another complication, even as wonderful as that.' He didn't move, and Ruby let him go; the touch of her cool hand lingered on his face. 'Are there many police about outside?'

'Five.'

He seemed to wince.

'I think they're mostly here to keep the crowds away,' Ruby went on. 'There are several hundred people in the street, walking up and down as if this were Southend on a Sunday afternoon. Two ice-cream salesboys must be making a fortune. I had to fight my way in.'

'They'll go, after dark.'

'And you'll try to escape then?'

'Yes,' said Dawlish, 'after I've talked to Hillman. I'll have to.'

Ruby was at the table again, unfastening an apron which hung on a hook, and she looked round with a queer smile, as if she had some secret which amused her.

'He's not living here any more.'

'*What?*' He actually forgot to keep his voice low.

'Hush!'

'Where is he? How do you know?'

'Mrs Flaherty, who lives on the first floor, has always stood in for Mrs Wattle at holiday times and highdays and holidays,' answered Ruby. 'I've just been talking to her. Hillman said that he was scared to stay where you might find him, and the police agreed that it might be a good idea if he went somewhere else. He packed all his things, his room's empty, and Mrs Flaherty doesn't know where he's gone.'

Dawlish ejaculated: 'Well, life goes on.'

'Pat,' said Ruby, 'if you can't find Hillman, you can't find out why he's doing this, can you?'

Dawlish didn't answer.

'And unless you want to give yourself up, there's no point in leaving here. Hillman's the one hope you have of finding out what it all means.' Ruby was very cool and logical, at any other time Dawlish would have paused to admire her complete detachment. 'Your friend Jeremy is too far away. There isn't any doubt that your wife will be watched everywhere she goes, and so will your other friends, in case you try to get in touch with them. The only wise thing is to stay here.'

'Except,' said Dawlish.

'Except what?' She was taking knives and forks out of a drawer, and laying the table, which ran on wheels. She did everything with quick efficiency, making hardly a sound. They kept their voices low, but Dawlish knew she would have told him had there been anyone else on this floor. The neighbour opposite was out for the afternoon and evening.

'If I stay here, I can't do anything at all,' said Dawlish. 'I'm suspected of a murder I didn't commit—remember? And the police don't take my side. If anyone is going to get results, I'll have to get them myself.'

'You've forgotten someone,' Ruby pointed out.

'Who?'

'Me.'

Dawlish stood up, and went towards her. He still did not understand her, although at times he believed that she was attracted to him with a kind of wilful infatuation. The way he caught her looking at him occasionally suggested that; and the way she had pursed her lips, kissed him, and said, 'Let's say it's love at first sight.'

'Ruby,' he said, 'I don't think I'm ever going to be able to say thanks for what you're doing, but don't hold out on me. I'm not in the mood. I know you're probably as much on edge as I am, but let's deal just with the situation, shall we? What do you mean?'

'I know where to find Hillman,' Ruby told him, and smiled brightly into his face. 'One of the things I found out was that Hillman shouldn't be overlooked—that was even before you told me what happened last night. I could imagine him scaring Marion, too. So I followed him once when he went to work—he usually left about half past ten.'

She was speaking very dryly, as if amused, and did not look away from Dawlish.

'Well?' he made himself ask quietly.

'He went to a pub in the Waterloo Road. It's called the Pack of Lies. I once asked him for a light, and he gave me a book of matches from the same pub. Judging from the hours he's away, he's a barman there.'

'Ah,' said Dawlish, very softly.

'I expect the police know where he is,' Ruby went on, 'and they'll be watching the Pack of Lies.'

'Could be,' agreed Dawlish, and added softly: 'I'll find out tonight.'

Ruby made no comment.

'And there's an advantage,' Dawlish went on. 'If I was on the run again, I could come back here.'

'You couldn't, and you know it,' Ruby said, flatly. It was as if she was consciously keeping emotion in check. 'You ought to stay here, and let me find out what Hillman knows. I shouldn't have told you where he's staying.' She spoke, suddenly sparked by anger. 'You can hide here for days, even for weeks, if necessary. If you're worried about your wife, I could tell her that you're all right. It wouldn't really be surprising if I went to see her, or telephone her, would it?'

'No,' agreed Dawlish.

'Then don't be a fool. Stay here in safety, and I'll see Hillman.'

'You've taken more than enough risks as it is,' Dawlish reminded her. 'Don't make any more.'

'What difference would it make to you?'

'If Hillman suspected you, he might kill you. It's as simple as that.'

'I see,' she said, and turned her back on him; in a way he had known Felicity do when she was in a huff. She was silent for a full minute, then turned and picked up a plate. She was pale, and her eyes were very bright. 'What you mean is that you're tired of my company, and would rather risk being caught than stay here. Why? Don't you think your wife would approve?'

17

TED

There was something peculiar about her.

There had been something odd about her sister, too.

Ruby was in the late twenties. She lived alone, and there was no indication that she had a man friend, certainly none that she was engaged. She was more than presentable, she was the type of tall, clean-limbed Englishwoman who would fascinate many men.

Why did she live alone?

Why had she taken such risks for him?

These thoughts flashed through Dawlish's mind, driving out the other obsessions. One thing was certain: he had to humour her. If this mood grew worse, she would become very difficult, and now that the other flats were occupied, raised voices would soon attract attention.

So he grinned across, and surprised her.

'Don't worry about Fel,' he said. 'She isn't the jealous kind. If I stayed here for a month, and as a result proved that Hillman had killed Mrs Wattle, Felicity would offer you the key of our front door for the rest of your life.'

Would those tactics work?

Ruby was obviously surprised, gave a little shrug and relaxed, pushing the table-trolley towards the middle of the room.

'She sounds rather nice.'

'She is very nice.'

'Lucky woman to have a husband who realises it.'

'I keep telling her,' said Dawlish, mildly. 'I also keep telling her how lucky she is to have a handsome hero like me, with a positive growing-finger for pigs and apples—'

'For *what?*'

Dawlish talked lightly about the pigs and the orchard at Four Ways, and Ruby seemed amused and genuinely interested. Her mood had changed, but it might change back when they started to discuss Hillman again. He had to go and find Hillman; the only question was whether he should go tonight or wait until tomorrow. Every hour of delay might be making the situation worse for him; but it might also give Hillman a better chance to get right out of reach.

With the police so intent on the case, Hillman wouldn't try, yet. If he vanished, suspicion would be bound to switch to him. He wasn't a fool, so rather than run far he would probably stay within call; Ruby was probably right in thinking that he was at the Pack of Lies, at Waterloo Road.

It wasn't yet eight o'clock and the earliest Dawlish could leave was eleven; it would be wise to stay until one o'clock, when no one was likely to be about—unless the police did decide to keep watch here.

Was there any point in their doing so?

With Hillman gone and the woman dead, would they think that anything was likely to attract Dawlish to Harven Street?

'Careful,' he warned himself. 'The police don't know that I know Hillman's left.'

So they might still expect him to come here, and might have the house watched day and night. They would not be deterred by the reasoning that no man in his senses would make a return visit to this house. Dawlish's whole life had been littered with instances of the absurd; they would reason that he might think that this was the last place he would come to; and so he would come.

Ruby was quite gay over supper.

Dawlish kept his end up, but on the bed behind her was the *Evening Globe*, with Felicity's face staring at him. Felicity would be tormenting herself with the questions which obsessed him.

Why had this happened?

Why had he been framed for murder?

Who wanted to see him hanged, or sent to prison for life?

'Ted,' said Felicity, as she handed Ted some coffee after dinner at the flat, 'I don't want you to send for Joan. I'd rather be here on my own. You can stay at your club, can't you?'

'Lord, yes. I'll run away the minute you say the word,' Ted assured her. He looked rather like a black St Bernard, although half an hour before she had caught him tugging at his thick hair with a comb. 'Can't say I like the idea of leaving you here on your own, though.'

'You needn't worry about me,' Felicity said, bitterly. 'The police watch every move I make.'

'There is that,' agreed Ted, gloomily. 'Hell of a situation, and I don't think I've done much to help. But I had to show you the worst.'

Felicity patted his hand.

'You've been fine.' She tried to be cheerful. 'And you've faced facts and tried to make me face them, too. It would have been better if Tim hadn't run away.'

'Easy,' protested Ted. 'Run away's a bit hard.'

Felicity put down her coffee, untasted, and jumped up.

'Oh, I can't settle for five minutes on end! I keep thinking there must be some obvious solution which I just can't see. I *know* Pat didn't do either of these things, I know he's not ill, and yet I can't see the answer.'

'Kind of abracadabra,' Ted commented lugubriously. 'I know exactly what you mean.' He appeared to brood, watching her as she bent down, picked up the coffee, drank it at one gulp.

'Ted, for heaven's *sake* don't sit there staring at me as if I were a freak!' she cried. 'I'm just a woman in love with her husband, and who doesn't think he's a killer and doesn't believe that he had a mistress tucked away! Even if he did he wouldn't choose a girl like Marion Ard. What on earth do you think has happened to him? That he's taken leave of his senses?'

As the words hovered on the air, she caught her breath. Ted didn't respond. Felicity raised a clenched hand, as if she wanted to strike him, as if she would strike anyone who came within reach.

'What's happened to *you*?' she demanded shrilly. 'It's you who've gone mad, not Pat. You've worked with him all your life, and so has Tim. You know him almost as well as I do. What makes you think he's suddenly become a different creature? He's good, don't you remember that? He's *good*, not bad. Anyone would think you knew as little about him as that cold-blooded Penfold. If ever I hated a man, it's Penfold.' She paused, but Ted just sat, and she drew a deep breath and went on gustily, angrily: 'Don't just sit there. You must have some reason for thinking Pat would behave like this, however crazy. Tell me what it is.'

Ted raised his hands, then dropped them heavily on to his knees.

'*Are you going to tell me?*' Felicity shouted.

'Take it easy, Fel,' Ted urged, and stood up clumsily. At his full height, he was massive and imposing; and a man on whom Pat had relied a hundred times.

'How do you expect me to take it easy when Pat's best friends are betraying him?'

'Dammit, Fel—'

She drew a deep breath, as if to shout again; but instead she bit her lips, turned round and went out into the kitchen. He heard her banging the crockery about, heard water splashing, knives and forks rattling. He sat staring moodily at the open door. Now and again he thought he heard a sob, but he didn't go in. She had been gone a quarter of an hour when at last she came back, looking very pale, without much lipstick or rouge. Her eyes were very bright; grey-green eyes which could laugh easily at normal times.

'I'm sorry,' she said. 'I'm over-tired, I suppose.'

'Fel,' Ted said.

'Hm-hm?'

'You're frightened, and so am I. Why don't you be honest with yourself?'

'I'm trying to be.'

'Has Pat been himself lately?'

'He was a bit tired before we went away, that's all. You may not realise it, but he was worried about me. I had a serious oper- ation, remember? I was in hospital for two months, and in a nursing home for another month. He—'

She caught her breath.

Ted's brown eyes looked unhappier than she had ever seen them.

'No,' she said in a hopeless, low-pitched voice. 'I just don't believe what you're thinking, that Pat had to find consolation while I was in hospital. We're talking about Pat, not some little cocksparrow of a man who loses his self-respect if he can't sleep with a woman every other night.'

Her words fell on to silence. Ted did not look away from her.

She shivered, and clasped her hands, then began to move about the flat, touching books, the telephone, a lamp, ornaments, the photograph; suddenly she snatched the photograph and stared at it, then swung round towards Ted.

'Have you forgotten this?'

'Fel,' said Ted, 'if I thought it would help, I'd lose my other leg for Pat. You know it.'

'I know one thing,' Felicity said, and was very tight-lipped as she faced him, and brought the photograph to him. 'You're keeping something back. You know something you haven't told me—or you *think* you know. What is it?'

'Fel—'

'What is it?'

'Oh, hell,' groaned Ted, and took the photograph and put it carelessly on the arm of the chair behind him. 'Well, I suppose you can't hate me any more than you do at the moment. Pat took a hell of a beating when you were in hospital. For two weeks there didn't seem much chance that you'd recover. You wouldn't know. Now and again he—now and again,' repeated Ted with great precision, 'he went wild. Stormed against fate, said if he lost you, he'd go crazy. He drank too much, too. And there wasn't much that Tim or I could do. The doctors were the only people who could help him. We'd never seen him like it, and it taught us a thing or two. First, how much he loved you, and second, how he'd been living on his nerves for a long time. That was always the trouble with Pat. He didn't look as if he was worried, ever; he could walk through an earthquake and talk as if nothing was going on, and for twenty years he's been using up all his reserves. That fantastic courage of his had to come from somewhere. Then the real danger to you seemed to make something crack inside him. It wouldn't surprise me at all if he had to do something, at that time, which he wouldn't normally dream of doing. Consolation is only a word. He probably thought that he was going mad, and needed something to help steady him. We couldn't, so—'

Ted broke off.

Felicity said in a pain-racked voice: 'How is it that I didn't know?'

'How could anyone tell you?' asked Ted, reasonably. 'You were at death's door for two weeks. It was a month after you got back to Four Ways before you could manage without a nurse, another two months before you were well enough to take this trip. There was no point in telling you about Pat, anyhow, because once you were on the mend, he was himself again. Seemed to be, anyhow. Happy as the proverbial sandboy, if a bit edgy. Fel, answer me this: didn't he jump at the chance of two months' cruise more quickly than you expected? Didn't he seem to need a rest almost as much as you?'

That was true.

More was true too; the way Pat had studied and brooded over Tim's letters at the various ports of call. It was almost possible to forget that she had really made him promise to help Marion Ard, he hadn't wanted to himself. Yet even that was out of character; normally he would have said that he could not stand by, that he would have to go and see if he could help the girl. Instead, he had fought against it until she, Felicity his wife, had pushed him into helping Marion Ard.

Felicity recalled that meeting in the drawing-room at Four Ways, and tried to remember any sign which might suggest that Pat had known the girl before. Marion Ard hadn't kept those big, limpid eyes off him, but Pat hadn't looked at her much, had turned and stared out of the window a great deal—almost as if he had been unable to meet the girl's eyes.

'One other thing,' Ted was going on. 'He didn't ask Bill Trivett what this was all about. Normally, he would have done. Obviously there was a possibility that if the Yard started to probe, they'd find out the truth. That's what Tim thinks. Talking of Tim, all right, he ran away: he told Osborne that it was to make sure that he couldn't be compelled to say or do anything that would harm Pat.'

In some ways that was the most dreadful fact of all.

'Ted,' said Felicity, slowly, deliberately, 'I do not believe that Pat knows anything about these murders, and I do not believe that he had ever seen Marion Ard before that day at Four Ways. I think it's time Tim came back, and time that you and he started to work on the assumption that Pat had nothing to do with this.'

Ted didn't speak.

'Sleep on it,' Felicity advised with forced brightness. 'Telephone me in the morning.'

Ted said awkwardly: 'Fel, I feel such a swine.'

'Good night,' she said, with the same brittle brightness.

When she went to the porch with him, she saw a policeman standing at the closed doors of the garage, opposite; the man made no attempt to conceal himself. Ted went limping down the steps, turned at the foot and waved; but he waved at a closing door.

Felicity went back to the big room, and picked up the photograph.

All logic and all reason was against her, and she was quite sure that no one else believed in Pat.

While Felicity was moving about the bedroom, telling herself that it was useless to get into bed, for she would never sleep, and while Dawlish and Ruby Ard were playing cribbage in the room at Harven Street, Detective-Inspector Penfold was sitting at his desk at the Yard, going through every report now available. He looked better than he had that morning, for he had slept for a few hours in the afternoon and early evening. During that time, hundreds of reports that Dawlish had been seen in different parts of the country had come in, and every one had to be considered, and checked. Alone in the big office, where there were four other desks, Penfold kept tapping his big white teeth with a pencil. He had the ability to concentrate absolutely on one thing at a time; just now he was concentrating on the likely places where Dawlish might hide.

Every place where he might go was being watched, and the telephone at Four Ways and at the mews flat were tapped.

He knew that Beresford had left the flat.

He pushed the reports aside, and began to review the case again, considering every person concerned in it. He considered the reports of Dawlish's 'anxiety period' after and during his wife's grave illness. He considered the fact that Mrs Wattle was the only positive witness to the fact that Dawlish had known the murdered girl, and also considered the fact that although the Yard had been working hard on it, no other witness had been found who had actually seen them together. Dawlish had probably known all there was to know about clandestine meetings. As far as Penfold could find out, there had been no written communications between him and Marion Ard.

Another man might have been satisfied to forget the first murder, in view of everything there was on the second, but Penfold was now examining everything simply with a view to finding Dawlish. He was nervous in case a senior officer was put on to the job; failure to find Dawlish might keep promotion back for years.

So he checked every note and every report sedulously, and it was nearly midnight before he finished. His was the only light on in the office, and it shone on him brightly, casting black shadows over his eyes and over his mouth.

He said aloud: 'It's damned queer about Ruby Ard. She went to live at Harven Street, and was waiting for Dawlish at Four Ways.'

He lit a cigarette.

'He couldn't have been having an *affaire* with *both* sisters, could he?'

He drew hard at the cigarette.

'Her room was searched last night and thoroughly searched this morning. Hm.' He rummaged through the reports and found one which said that the men who had searched the Harven Street house had 'entered Flat 6 which was empty. Ruby Ard had obviously just woken up.'

'Obviously?'

At this time last night, Penfold had been quite sure in his own mind that Dawlish had got away from the house but not the district. He had checked the precautions closely, and did not see how any man could have got through the cordon. Dawlish was a strong and resourceful man, but he wasn't another Houdini.

Penfold thought: 'Would it be worth another look? He might frighten her into letting him stay. If he isn't there she'd be mad at being woken up, but if we did catch him there—'

He broke off.

He smiled a little, thin-lipped, for he was in no mood for smiling. He could tell himself that it was only a matter of time before Dawlish was found, but the fact remained that he was in danger of getting a black mark; an unbroken run of success was what he wanted, and meant to get.

'There's a man at the back and one at the front,' he said, standing up. 'I needn't take anyone else.'

He put on his hat, and went out.

18

NIGHT

Ruby was still awake, Dawlish knew.

The only light came from the stairs, for it was after midnight, and window lights had been out for some time. The house and the gardens were silent, not even a cat disturbed the quiet. In the distance he heard the occasional beat of a car engine.

He was sitting up, a cushion behind his head, his legs up on a chair. It was chillier than last night, and a blanket was draped round him. Ruby lay on her bed, and there was none of the steady, rhythmic breathing he had heard when he had been sure that she was asleep.

He was looking out of the window, and turned to face her. He saw that her eyes were open, for a faint gleam of reflected light was on them.

'Hallo, Pat,' she whispered.

'Hi.'

'You're not comfortable.'

'I'm fine.'

'Why don't you come and rest properly?'

'I'm fine, Ruby.'

'You're a fool,' she said, in the same whispering voice, and he could imagine that she was smiling at him; certainly she was not in that taut, difficult mood. 'Most men would think so, too.'

'Why don't you go to sleep, Ruby?'

'I can't, for thinking about you,' she said. 'I don't often share a room with a man.'

What answer was there to that?

'I don't know how long you'll be able to keep away from the police,' Ruby went on, 'but I shouldn't think it would be too long, would you? And once they arrest you, you'll have to be on your own for a long time. Even if you were found not guilty—' She paused for a moment, and her voice hardened: 'You aren't guilty, are you?'

'No,' answered Dawlish, solemnly.

'You'll have to spend a lot of lonely nights, whether you are or not. Just think, this might be your last chance of company for months.'

He pushed the blanket off his legs, and the chair creaked. He grunted as he got up. She moved over to the other side of the bed and he went across to her, searching for her hands; they were very cool, and clutched his tightly.

'Ruby,' he said, 'I've learned just one thing that seems to matter, and that is—never do today what you might regret tomorrow.'

'You'll never regret me, Pat.'

He squeezed her hands.

'No,' he agreed, 'I'd never regret you. But you might have a lot of regrets about me. If I get through this, if we should ever have an *affaire* when there aren't any compelling circumstances like these, then—wonderful. But not now, Ruby. If you'd rather, I'll leave right away. There's a sound chance of avoiding the man at the back.'

'No!' she exclaimed. 'No, you mustn't go until they take the guards away.' She clutched his hands very tightly. 'Go and sit back again, and forget what a fool I am, forget it.' She pushed him away, and he stepped cautiously to the chair, wondering how long a reprieve he had gained, and what was really in her mind. Man and woman, here together—who could blame her, and who could blame him?

He found himself smiling, secure because she could not see his expression.

No one would have any cause to blame him.

At most, he must stay here tomorrow, and he still had to make up his mind now whether it would be wiser to leave at once. He didn't know where to go, except that he was sure that it must not be to any place where he was known. His size was his great handicap; people would look up, see a 'big man', and as often as not go to the nearest policeman.

Wherever he went, what could he do?

The only man who might be able to help was Hillman, who was probably at the Pack of Lies. It would be a long business, anyhow. If he let himself dream of getting hold of Hillman, where could he take him and keep him long enough to frighten him into telling the truth?

Dawlish thought: 'It can't be done.'

And he could not stay here.

If only he could see Felicity, and talk to her for an hour.

He heard a car approaching along the main road, and listened, very wideawake, in case it came this way. It did. Now it was travelling along the road which led to Harven Street and several others which were parallel. If it were going to turn this corner, it should change gear now.

He heard the different note of the lower gear.

He found himself tensing, and stood up; the chair creaked.

'What is it?' whispered Ruby.

'There's a car coming this way.'

'A lot of people have cars.'

He heard it approaching, and knew that it was slowing down; a moment later, he heard it stop; so it was close to this house. He went to the door, unbolted and unlocked it, and opened it an inch. Ruby was sitting up in bed. He could see the lighted staircase and shiny linoleum; that was all. Then a door opened downstairs, and he heard footsteps. There were two men. It must be nearly one o'clock, and only one man lived in this house, so these were probably police.

Where were they coming?

'Why should they come here now?' Ruby demanded.

'If they find me, tell them I forced you to give me shelter, that I threatened you,' Dawlish whispered urgently.

'But—'

'They might be going to Mrs Wattle's room, or to Hillman's.' Dawlish told himself. They came up the first flight of stairs, proving that Hillman's was the more likely. Dawlish heard them on the landing, then on the next flight of stairs.

'They're coming here!' Ruby whispered, in sudden panic.

Dawlish closed the door, turned the lock with infinite caution and heard the men reach the landing below.

'The window,' Ruby gasped.

'No,' said Dawlish. 'Lie down. If they bang on the door don't answer at once, let them bang two or three times.'

'*What are you going to do?*'

He didn't answer. The men were close to the head of the stairs now, and were not talking. They reached the landing, and Dawlish felt quite sure that they were coming here. They stopped just outside, and banged on the door—with their knuckles. Dawlish thought. Ruby was sitting bolt upright, and seemed to be holding her breath. The man knocked again, and called:

'Sorry to disturb you, Miss Ard. This is Inspector Penfold.'

With one other man, Dawlish reminded himself; and the fact that there were only two of them outside had put new hope into his mind.

'What—what is it?' Ruby asked, in a choky voice.

'Open the door, miss, please.'

'*Go out of the window!*' Ruby whispered.

Dawlish didn't answer.

'Miss Ard, please open the door.' Penfold became sharp-voiced, and gave the door an extra thump; as if he had heard the whispering.

'Just—just a minute!'

Ruby began to scramble off the bed. Dawlish stepped to the door, and stood on the other side, pressing close to the wall. His heart hammered furiously. He saw Ruby pick up a dressing-gown. There was just enough light for him to make out the shape of her face and the strange brilliance of her eyes. She turned the key, and he could tell that her hand was trembling. He took the key from her as he stood within two feet of the door, pressed against the wall and breathing very softly.

Ruby opened the door.

'What—what do you want? What are you doing here at this time of night?'

'Sorry, Miss Ard,' said Penfold formally. 'We'd just like to ask you one or two questions.' The light from the landing shone fully on to Ruby, and Dawlish saw her vividly, and could tell the depth of her distress.

Penfold strode in.

Another man blocked the doorway.

'We won't keep you—' Penfold began, and then he glanced round and saw Dawlish.

* * *

'*My God*,' Penfold breathed.

'Hallo, Inspector,' said Dawlish, politely. 'I thought you'd catch up with me before long. Here's one possible victim I haven't killed.'

'Stay where you are,' ordered Penfold. 'Mickle, go and summon—'

'Soon,' said Dawlish.

He moved much too fast for Penfold, who was a bulkier, heavier man. He saw Penfold shoot out his fists to try to fend him off, but grabbed the detective's right arm, and twisted; Penfold gasped with pain. Dawlish twisted again, and sent the Yard man staggering across the room, towards the window. The man in the door had a whistle at his lips, and was backing away; Dawlish could see the whites of his eyes. Dawlish leapt at him, and the first *peep* of the whistle was strangled. Dawlish struck the man savagely in the stomach, grabbed his arm and hustled him into the room. Penfold was just straightening up. Dawlish, still outside, pulled the door, and closed it on the two men with surprising quiet. Penfold bellowed, '*Here!*' Dawlish turned the key in the lock, then swung round and raced down the stairs. He reached the hall while Penfold was still shouting, and the two Yard men banged wildly on the locked door, he heard no one else. He pulled open the front door, and saw a car standing right outside. No one else was about. He went straight to the car, and, some distance along saw a policeman; but the man could hear nothing of the shouting, and he did not hurry. Dawlish slammed the door. The key wasn't in the dashboard, he couldn't have all the luck. He took out his own keys, and used an ignition master-key; by the time the constable had drawn near, the ignition was glowing red.

'All right, sir?' the policeman called.

''Night,' grunted Dawlish.

The man stepped nearer. Suspiciously? Dawlish eased off the

brakes and started off, not too fast; he did not know the controls, and did not want to jolt the car and alarm the constable, who might hear the shouting at any moment.

Penfold was probably out of the bedroom by now.

Dawlish reached the corner.

Within minutes, the call would be out for Penfold's car; within minutes, every police patrol would be on the lookout for it, and soon every policeman on his beat would be watching out, too. Dawlish shot forward towards the main road. While he was in this he had only a few minutes' grace; in another car, he would have hope. He remembered the parked cars along the street parallel with Harven Street, and turned down there; three cars were drawn up at the side of the road. He passed an old Austin 7, which would be too small for him, next to this was an oldish Humber Hawk. He pulled up in front of it, and switched off his engine. The other car was locked, but his key should open it. He fought to prevent his hands from trembling as he took the key, thrust it into the keyhole and began to twist. It did not catch easily. If he couldn't open this car and start the engine, he had thrown away what chance he had.

There hadn't been much anyhow.

He felt the key take hold, twisted and heard the lock go back. He gulped as he slid into the seat. His knees were tight against the dashboard, for the seat was in position for a short driver. He found the control handle, depressed it and eased the seat backwards. No lights appeared on the driving mirror, and as yet he had not heard the police whistle.

The ignition was easier to force than the door lock.

He pressed the self-starter, and the engine turned over at once. He drove towards the far end of the street, and as he reached it, fancied that he heard the blast of a police whistle. He turned the corner and raced towards the main road, which was brightly lit, and crossed it; as he reached the side streets on the other side, he switched on the lights.

He was out of the most dangerous area now.

He was still in Kensington, heading towards the river, on the other side of which, near Waterloo Bridge, Hillman was at the Pack of Lies—if Ruby knew what she was talking about.

Dawlish drove a little less furiously.

Two or three cars were parked in a wide street when he saw the headlights of another flashing at cross-roads; that would be a police car, already summoned. He pulled in to the side of the road, and switched off the lights; the police car swung round this corner and hurtled towards him. He bent as low as he could. The police car flashed by, towards the main road, and as it turned another corner, Dawlish started off again.

He reached the Embankment and drove along it as far as Lambeth Bridge, then crossed the Thames. The brightly lit face of Big Ben seemed to be overlording the sleeping city. The lights on Westminster Bridge reflected on the water, like the lamps on the Embankment. He slowed down, for he was in no immediate danger here.

The danger would be at the Pack of Lies, which might be guarded by the police.

19

THE PACK OF LIES

As he reached Waterloo Road, and turned right towards the public-house, Dawlish had decided what danger he was most likely to face. None of the places being watched could have a strong guard on them, and none would be fully equipped to tackle him if he arrived, but all would be ready to send for help, by telephone or radio. He would be seen to go into the pub, and a report would be flashed to the Yard; so the danger would be on getting out, not getting in.

He saw the inn sign, still illuminated in red neon. He drove past it, and saw a man in plain-clothes standing in a doorway opposite; just one man. He drove quite slowly, turned the next corner, then reversed in the road. No one was about. He went back, more slowly this time. The man who had been standing in the doorway had stepped on to the pavement, and was near the kerb. He was smoking and looked bored. Dawlish looked right and left, and saw no one else; why should there be, at the front? There might be another man at the side of the house, that was all.

He slowed down, and wound down the window.

'Excuse me,' he said.

The man came forward, promptly enough. Dawlish depressed the handle and, as the man reached the car, thrust the door open. He heard a gasp and a scuffle of footsteps. He was out of the car in a flash, while the man staggered back. He caught his right arm, twisted him round and thrust his arm upwards in a hammer lock; as the man gasped, he said harshly:

'Don't shout, if you want to live.'

He propelled the man towards the doorway where he had been standing, and as he reached the doorway, sensed that the other was going to fight back. He released the wrist and crooked both hands round the man's neck; he actually felt the cry for help coming, and stifled it.

He tightened his pressure.

Soon, the man went limp, and Dawlish let him go, supporting him with one arm.

He looked up and down, and saw three cars coming from the other side of the river, all with their headlights on; there was a roar of three engines. Were these police, coming to the Pack of Lies because the alarm had been raised? The second car was an open sports model with a man and girl in front, man and girl at the back; and he heard them singing. All three cars flashed by.

Dawlish hustled the unconscious man to the back of the car, and lifted him in. He used the man's own tie to bind his wrists, and handkerchief to gag him. He felt his pulse, and made sure that it was beating.

Dawlish had never felt calmer or more collected.

He realised that from the doorway one could see both the front and the side entrances of the Pack of Lies; probably only one man had been stationed there, as a precaution against the outside chance, rather than the expectation, that Dawlish would arrive. Dawlish walked across the road, and took the side street. The side door had glass panels. He bent his elbow and cracked it against the glass; it broke with a loud report, and there was a sharp pain at his elbow. He ignored that, and pulled cautiously at long splinters of glass sticking in the sides of the window. He removed enough to make a hole sufficiently large to put his hand and arm through, then groped for the key. He was lucky, for it was there, and the bolt and chain were in the middle of the door. He made little noise, but did not let the risk of noise deter him too much.

He opened the door, and no one appeared to have heard him.

He stepped inside and closed the door, then shone his pencil torch. A flight of stairs led straight up from the end of this passage. There was a heavy smell of beer, and crates were piled up alongside the stairs. A door leading to one of the bars was open, and the brass of beer handles and the glass of bottles and glasses shimmered in light which came from the street.

He went upstairs.

This was a low building; there could be only two floors above the ground, and the top one was probably little more than an attic. He went up, and reached a landing with five doors leading off.

How many people slept in this house?

He opened one door, very softly; and it was an empty parlour. Next to it was an empty bedroom. On the other side were kitchen and bathroom, also empty. There were two more doors down here; after them he would have to explore whatever rooms were above his head. He saw a flight of stairs even narrower than the top flight at Harven Street, and which would be much creakier, and make a great deal of noise.

He opened the next door; in the light from a street lamp outside he saw a man and woman sleeping on a double bed, the man's arm dangling over the side, and almost touching the floor. The key was on the inside of the lock. Dawlish took it out, closed and then locked the door, and turned towards the next room.

As he touched the handle, a bright light came on, dazzling him. As he spun round towards the stairs, a man said:

'Don't move, or I'll shoot you.'

The man was standing halfway down the stairs leading to the top floor, and carried some kind of gun. The light was immediately above Dawlish's head, shining right on to his eyes; and at first all he could see was a shadowy figure, and that pointing weapon. He did not know how long it had taken him to recover from the shock and the glare, but soon he was able to see clearly, so it could not have been more than a few seconds.

The man covering him was Hillman.

Hillman seemed as if he could not believe what he saw; stood looking astounded, but holding the gun very still, and covering Dawlish. When Dawlish moved, Hillman spoke again in a high-pitched voice:

'Don't move!' There was a pause. 'It can't be Dawlish.' He gulped. 'On a plate,' he breathed, and raised the gun; there was no doubt that he was going to shoot.

He was absolutely justified in doing so.

He could shoot to kill, and it would not be murder; would be considered justifiable homicide.

He was grinning.

Dawlish said: 'What are you getting out of this, Hillman? What good's it doing you?'

'You'd be surprised,' Hillman answered, and his thin, swarthy face was twisted in a smile of gloating delight. 'But you'll never know.'

He fired.

Dawlish flung himself to one side.

The bullet caught him in the shoulder, with such force that

he swung round. He had little choice: had to rush at Hillman, who was standing high above him, and would shoot to kill; or to turn and run. Either way, he hadn't much chance. He knew that the man was about to shoot again, actually saw the gun lowered, towards his legs.

Then a woman from behind Hillman screamed: 'What's going on?'

Hillman half turned towards her. Dawlish snatched a broken bottle from a crate with his right hand, and flung it at the man, saw Hillman dodge, saw the woman behind him. The dream vanished, taking with it all hope of talking to Hillman, or forcing him to go with him long enough to learn the truth. Dawlish flung another bottle, as he turned to run down the stairs. No matter what he attempted, it went wrong; it was as if he was fated to fail.

He heard Hillman gasp, and the woman scream. He glanced round and saw Hillman falling; the bottle must have smacked hard against his head—but he might recover quickly, and the woman was glaring at Dawlish. He ran down the stairs, his left shoulder numb, and his elbow painful. He reached the passage, and the side door. There were confused sounds behind him, but none of Hillman running after him; could the man be unconscious? Dawlish reached the street and the corner, and everywhere seemed quiet and deserted. He raced towards the car which stood with its side-lights on; and in the distance was another car. Police? He got in, started the engine and moved off slowly. He had to press his left arm against his side now, and do nearly all the work with his right hand and arm.

Where?

If he gave himself up . . .

He saw the other car approach, draw level and pass. The only thing which stopped him from waiting for the police was some instinctive faith, and inability to believe that he was really finished, yet he could see no hope anywhere. He drove towards Waterloo Bridge. Two taxis came towards him. The lights shimmered on the water, and somewhere a tug's engine was throbbing. He drove straight over the bridge, then towards the West End, which was nearly deserted, although here and there were signs of life; couples, cabs, policemen. He went towards the mews flat, the place which had been his and Felicity's honeymoon home, the place where Felicity might be. It was like a homing instinct. He felt the warmth of his own blood at his shoulder, arm and elbow; pain was nagging at him all the time. He wondered how much damage had been done. He passed two police cars heading in the other direction, feeling numbed, and hardly able to think; but thoughts seeped into his mind. If anything was certain, it was that the mews flat would be watched, because every policeman at the Yard knew that was where he might go.

He reached Piccadilly.

He would be near Curzon Street in five minutes, at the flat in six.

If he could see Felicity just once, it would help; he must see her before he was caught, and the whole insane business of trial began.

He turned down towards Curzon Street, and then towards the mews. Every light approaching it and every light in the mews itself was on; of course, the police were making sure that no one could approach unobserved. He turned into the mews. It seemed empty. He switched on the headlights, and they picked out a man standing close to the wall halfway along, nearly opposite the flat itself.

There was a light on in the flat.

He drove past the front door, towards more flats at the far end; and then swung the wheel. He saw the solitary figure leap towards the right, as if afraid of being pinned against the wall. He stopped the car and opened the door with his right hand as a police whistle shrilled out; there would be other police nearby, waiting to rush here.

He got out.

He heard a grunting sound at the back of the car; the man he had brought from the Pack of Lies was trying to attract attention.

Dawlish felt weak and silly, and felt blood running down his arm, and into his hand; he flexed his fingers, as if that would help to stop it. The whistle shrilled out, but the man was backing away towards the exit, not wanting to give battle. He'd be a fool if he did.

Then the door of the flat opened.

Dawlish looked up, and saw Felicity.

20

HOME

Felicity saw him standing at the foot of the steps, looking so huge and massive, holding his left arm limply by his side, and staring towards her in a strange, mute appeal. She heard the whistle shrill out again, and saw the detective blowing it, twenty yards away from Pat.

Pat had a funny kind of smile at his lips, and he moved towards her.

She started down to him.

'Stay there,' he called; she had heard that tone of voice before, and knew that he was in pain. 'Get ready to shut the door.' He reached the steps and came up them fairly quickly, but looked as if it took him all his time to keep steady. Felicity stood by the wide-open door, staring at his face, and the strange smile on it. 'Hallo, Fel,' he said, in that taut, hurt voice. 'Must have a talk to you.'

She put out a hand to take his right and glancing down saw the red on his left hand, and red spots on the steps and on the little landing.

'Just a scratch,' he said; it was the kind of disclaimer he was bound to make. He stepped past her, brushing against her, and she still had an impression that there was a peaceful look in his eyes. 'Close the door,' he went on. 'I'll talk to them in a minute. Any whisky in the house?'

'Pat,' she said, in a strangled voice.

'Don't worry,' he said. 'It'll be all right. I had to see you.'

She closed the door on the sound of car engines.

'Here comes the law,' he announced. 'Properly blotted my copybook this time. If I had two sound arms I'd do a Sydney Street on them, but you wouldn't like that, my darling, would you? Any luck with that drink?'

She hated to leave him, even for a moment, but hurried ahead to the room where she and Ted had sat talking a few hours ago. She was still fully dressed. Dawlish went to the window which overlooked the mews, opened it an inch and startled her by the power in his voice:

'*You out there!*' There was a pause. '*If anyone tries to get in, I'll break his neck. I'll come out in half an hour.*'

At least two cars were at the end of the mews, at least eight men had heard him.

'*Just keep away from me,*' he roared. '*Give me half an hour.*'

They wouldn't wait for long, but would undoubtedly be very cautious, assuming that he was mad enough to try to shoot his way out. He turned to Felicity, took the tumbler from her, sipped and then drank. 'Ah, that's good. You look good, too. Hallo, my darling.'

She was deep-tanned from the weeks of warm sun, and her eyes were very bright, clear even from anxiety at this moment; as if his coming had taken away the worst of her fears.

'Hallo, my darling,' she said in turn, and looked down at his hand. 'Come into the bathroom, I must do something to that arm.'

'It can wait. The police are very civilized, they'll patch me up before they send me down.'

'Come along,' Felicity insisted.

'Yes, dear,' Dawlish followed her into the bathroom, but obviously every step he took was an effort. He sat on the edge of the bath, near the taps, so that he could lean against the wall with his left side over the bath. 'One bullet and some glass, nothing much. Sorry.' He moved so that she could pull the coat off. The sight of blood did not worry either of them.

'I'll get a sponge,' Felicity said. 'How long do you think it'll be before the police come?'

'They'll surround the place first, and then they'll try sweet reason,' surmised Dawlish. 'They're taking it for granted that I'm loco, so they'll assume that I might try to fight to the death.' He grinned, but his teeth were clenched.

There was one gash at the elbow, not very deep; it was hardly bleeding. The bullet had caught him fairly high on the shoulder, and he did not think that the bone was damaged.

Felicity was very gentle.

'Fel,' he said, 'I didn't kill either of them.'

'Of course you didn't, don't be silly.'

'Bless you,' he said very softly. 'I've been trying to find out who did, and I hid in the little flat that Marion Ard's sister has at Harven Street.' He saw Felicity look up. 'A certain Ruby Ard,' he went on. 'She might know more than she pretends. She was all deep understanding, but I certainly didn't understand her. Either she's a nymphomaniac who hides her weakness well, or she took a love philtre, or else she thought she could find out whether I'd killed her sister if she offered me her charms.'

'Don't talk for the sake of talking, darling.'

'You bet I won't. I advised her to say I kept her at her flat by threats and force—that's her one hope of keeping out of trouble with the police. I didn't use force, though. She wanted me to stay. But the real angle they want is Hillman.'

Felicity went on sponging.

'Listen carefully, sweetheart,' Dawlish continued. 'I don't know for sure about Ruby Ard, but I do know that Hillman is working for someone else. I saw him tonight—this is his bullet. I'm pretty sure he's being paid for it. I know that he killed Mrs Wattle, no one else could have done. That's the line for the defence: that Hillman was in her room, that he had as great a chance to kill Mrs Wattle as I did.'

'You broke his nose,' Felicity said. 'Pat—'

Dawlish found himself grinning. 'I hit it hard enough, anyhow. If I had a chance I'd break his neck. I probably would have. Fel, he killed Mrs Wattle. I think he probably killed Marion Ard. Tell Ted and Tim.'

'I will,' Felicity promised.

She took a hand towel from the side of the bath, folded it into a pad, and then pressed it against the bullet wound, which was blue and puffy round the edges and which hurt a little; but this would stop the bleeding.

There was a ring at the front-door bell.

'They're on the way,' Dawlish said. 'Fel, what's the matter?'

He saw the fear back in her eyes as she said:

'Pat, I thought of Hillman, he was the obvious possibility, and I *told* Ted. But Ted thinks you did it. So does Tim. Tim got out of the country because he didn't want to risk being held for questioning, and having to give the police a lead. He says he found out that you knew Marion Ard.'

Dawlish looked bewildered.

'*Tim* found out? Is he crazy? He told me he'd gone hunting; there was a note at Four Ways.'

'I only know what Ted seems to think Tim agrees about,'

Felicity said. 'They say that you weren't yourself while I was in hospital, that you did some queer things.'

The bell rang again.

'Bolt that door, sweet,' Dawlish said now very softly, and Felicity turned and did so. Then she stood in front of him, and he studied her closely, every precious line of her face.

'You bet I did some queer things,' he agreed. 'I thought I'd lost you. Several times I got drunk. It was the damnedest thing. I can usually carry my liquor. Remember?' He actually twisted his lips into a smile. 'Well, either I drank much more than usual or I couldn't carry it properly. I got roaring drunk. And I was ready to take on the world. Fel, I thought I was losing you.'

Her eyes were strangely bright.

The bell rang again, and they heard banging on the outside door.

With his right hand, Dawlish gripped Felicity's arm, and drew her to him.

'What else, Fel?'

'They think—they think Marion Ard was a help to you, while I was in hospital.'

'Oh-h,' he said softly, and there was new tension in his smile. 'So that's the theory. No, Fel. Nothing like that then, nothing now, nothing ever.'

'Of course there wasn't!'

'Bless you,' Dawlish said, and had to force himself to go on: 'Fel, make them see sense.' He paused. 'What the hell's got into them—into Tim and Ted? It doesn't add up.' Felicity didn't speak, and Dawlish went on in a stronger voice: 'It would make sense only if they feel absolutely sure they're right, wouldn't it?'

'Yes,' Felicity managed to say.

'Fel, listen.' His fingers bit deep into her arm. 'See them. Persuade them they're wrong. Make them find out who convinced them. He's the answer. Put them on to Hillman, too. Don't ever let up on Hillman. If they find me guilty they might not hang me, but they might as well. Hillman and whoever persuaded Tim and Ted are the only hopes.'

Felicity almost said: 'You persuaded them.'

There was a heavy thud on the door outside, and suddenly Dawlish heard sounds outside the small window in the bathroom. Beyond the frosted glass he saw the beams of torches darting to and fro; several men were in the tiny garden. If he or Felicity didn't open a door soon, the police would break one down.

'Tell them it may be the only chance,' Dawlish urged. 'First Ruby, then Hillman, then Mr Persuasion. Fel, do you hear me?'

'Yes,' she said, chokily, 'yes, of course.' And in a moment she was clinging to him, and he could feel her fighting to keep her composure. The men outside were calling loudly, and there was a great banging at both the back and the front. A window crashed in. Dawlish heard men thumping inside the flat. He held Felicity tightly with his one sound arm, and did not speak.

A man called: 'Dawlish!'

Dawlish didn't answer.

'I *saw* him come in,' a second said.

Dawlish called: 'I'm here, I won't be a minute.' He didn't want to make Felicity ease away from him; wanted to give her all the comfort that he could. That was a joke; that he could comfort her. At least the pain in his shoulder was not so great.

A man banged on the front door.

'Are you in there, Dawlish?'

'Yes,' called Dawlish and squeezed Felicity fiercely, then eased the pressure of her body against his. 'Half a mo'!' He looked into Felicity's red and tear-stained eyes, and kissed her; then he stood up and moved to one side.

It was Felicity who unlocked the door.

Outside was Penfold; by his side was one of the biggest Flying Squad men; behind them, four other men, each one massive. Dawlish could not help himself; he grinned at Penfold.

'Brought some friends?' he asked as if inanely. 'Let 'em all come.' Felicity was close to him, and his right arm was round her shoulders; but the police were staring at his left shoulder. 'Blame Hillman,' he said. 'That man's a bad man. Did he tell you he killed Mrs Wattle?'

Then Penfold asked an incredible question.

'Are you Patrick Dawlish?' he demanded in a hard voice.

Dawlish gaped.

'Er,' he said blankly. 'That's me.'

'Patrick Dawlish, it is my duty to arrest you and to inform you that you are charged with the wilful murder of one Anna May Wattle at 43 Harven Street in the Royal Borough of Kensington...'

Penfold went on to the bitter end.

Dawlish said: 'No, oh, no,' and began to laugh, in a queer high-pitched way. 'Hark, Fel. He's repeating the formula. Am I Patrick Dawlish? *Am I Patrick Dawlish?*' He laughed again. 'They *pay* him for behaviour like this.'

'. . . quietly, please,' Penfold was saying.

'He must see a doctor at once,' Felicity said.

'We'll look after him, ma'am,' promised Penfold, and looked at Dawlish oddly. Two of his men moved forward, and one of them thrust out his hands. Dawlish felt the sharp cold of handcuffs on his right wrist, and knew that he was held fast to the largest man present.

Felicity did not speak again.

'I'll be all right,' Dawlish told her. He moved away, and his legs seemed to buckle, he would have fallen but for the support of the big man. Another man moved to help support him.

'Better get an ambulance,' Penfold said, almost regretfully.

*   *   *

Dawlish was grateful for a doctor and a nurse who behaved as if they did not care whether he was held on a murder charge or a parking offence. They were briskly competent. The doctor gave him an injection, to Penfold's obvious dissatisfaction, although the Yard man did not argue. After that, Dawlish had only pleasant sensations at first, as if he were floating away into the distance, and then as if the sun was setting; and then oblivion.

Ted Beresford, bright eyed, and more vigorous looking than he had been on the previous day, watched Felicity as she explained exactly what had happened. It was half past three in the morning, and she had just telephoned him. He had seen the bloodstains in the bathroom, the broken window, all the evidence of what had happened. He listened to what she said of Dawlish's message, and did not look away from her as she went on:

'There isn't the slightest doubt, Ted; he didn't kill either of them. Don't tell me he wasn't right in the head. He was weak from loss of blood and a bit hysterical, and if you'd heard Penfold ask him if his name was Patrick Dawlish, well, you would have burst your sides. It was ludicrous; the man's the most pompous fool I've ever known at the Yard. But the thing is, Pat didn't *do* it. He said that you and Tim had to work on Ruby Ard and Hillman, and find out who it was persuaded you that he was guilty. He said someone must have been working on you.'

'No one could,' Ted said.

'They must have been!'

Ted said. 'I'll get Tim back as soon as it's possible, and we'll work on Hillman. I expect the police will watch him pretty closely, but we'll find a way of making him talk. This Ruby Ard . . .' he shrugged. 'Why don't you see her in the morning, and see what you make of her?'

'I will, believe me,' said Felicity fervently. 'Ted, sleep on the couch, will you? I don't feel like being left alone again tonight.'

'Of course,' Ted acquiesced, and squeezed her arm. 'Now you turn in. Pat'll be well looked after.'

He watched her go into the bedroom, poured himself a whisky and soda, and sat drinking it until her room light went out. Then he punched some pillows into position, and stretched out on the large couch. There was a slight draught from the broken window, but that did not worry him. He went to sleep at last; and sleeping snored faintly.

A bang at a door woke him.

He opened his eyes on the instant, for he could sleep as lightly as Dawlish, and listened; he heard footsteps on the cobbles of the mews, and realised that it had been something at the front door: the postman or the newspapers. He lay for a few minutes, got up, stretched and yawned and glanced at the bedroom, hoping that Felicity was still asleep. Then he went to the front door. There were no letters but the two newspapers were on the mat. He wondered what they would say about the night's excitements, and whether they would report Pat's arrest. He found himself picturing Felicity's face, as she had insisted that Pat had not done this thing, and as she had told him that he must find out everything that Hillman knew.

And the persuader. . . .

He picked up the *Daily Globe* and opened it.

THIRD MURDER IN DAWLISH CASE

the headline screamed,

AFTER FIGHT WITH DAWLISH

Ted thought: 'Oh, God, oh, no!'

He read on:

'Oh, God,' he repeated. 'Pat.'

He read the article, looking like a granite figure: how Hillman had been found at the foot of the stairs at the Pack of Lies, with his carotid artery cut by broken glass from a beer bottle; he had bled to death. The story told how Dawlish had been identified by several people, including the woman who had been sleeping in the room next to Hillman when Dawlish had broken in.

Penfold went in to see Dawlish in hospital an hour after he had come round, when he had eaten a light breakfast, and been washed but not shaved by a nurse who showed much less friendliness than the nurse of the night before.

'Now let's have the whole truth from the beginning,' Penfold said without preamble. 'Start right back at the time when you first met Marion Ard.'

'The next time I say a word to you, it will be with my solicitor present,' Dawlish said.

'It won't make any difference,' Penfold declared almost wearily. 'Who do you want? This man Osborne?'

'My own man is Gayforth, of Lincoln's Inn.'

'He's in America,' Penfold told him. 'Dawlish, why don't you throw your hand in? Everyone can see that you're a sick man. God knows I don't want to minimise what you've done, but if there are any extenuating circumstances—'

'Inspector,' Dawlish said, 'I don't know who killed Marion Ard. I do know that Hillman killed Mrs Wattle. I wanted to try to frighten her into telling me the truth. I found my address in her flat, and I found out that Hillman paid no rent, which implies a close association—'

'She was his mistress,' Penfold said, 'and it makes no difference. We're not blind, Dawlish. We found your name and address there, too. Hillman said he wrote it down for her when he recognised you, some weeks ago. Blackmail was being considered, but that still doesn't affect the issue.'

'She told me that Hillman had forced her to lie about my knowing Marion Ard,' Dawlish growled. 'Why don't you open your ears to me? Hillman came and tried to attack me, and Mrs Wattle was alive in the room when I got away from him. Hillman's your man.'

The look on Penfold's face was almost frightening.

Penfold said bleakly: 'You killed Hillman last night by throwing a broken bottle at him. The point pierced the carotid artery.'

Dawlish caught his breath; then very slowly, all the colour faded from his face. He remembered that strangled cry and the way Hillman had fallen; he could see the woman's horror. He did not utter a word, even when Penfold spoke again. He sat up in bed, staring straight ahead of him, when Penfold closed the door.

Penfold went straight to the doctor in charge.

'Do you think there's any chance that he could act without knowing what he was doing?' he asked.

'If I were you I'd leave that kind of question to the defence,' the doctor said. 'I'd call him sane.'

21

GUILTY BUT . . .

Felicity looked into Osborne's good-looking, sun-tanned face, into his bright, confident eyes. He was standing in front of her in the big room at the mews flat. The broken window was behind him, patched up with stiff board. Ted sat back in a huge easy chair, and the photograph of him and Dawlish in uniform was back where it had come from. The piano was open.

'. . . In the face of new evidence, Mrs Dawlish, I have had reluctantly to conclude, from everything that Mr Beresford and Mr Jeremy have told me about your husband, that the defence must argue that he had been suffering from a mental illness, due perhaps to years of accumulated strain. Your own grave illness merely served to sharpen the effect, it was not the cause of it. Now I believe that it would be quite possible to work on the assumption that the jury, confronted with the evidence that we can produce, will in fact accept that fact of this temporary—er—poor mental balance. I'm afraid it's the one reasonable hope for Mr Dawlish. I have no doubt that a dozen specialists could be found to submit an expert opinion in your husband's favour.

There is also what you tell me about what happened last night, and the way in which Mr Dawlish laughed in the face of the officer who arrested him. I know that you may dismiss that lightly, but in court, faced with such a question and knowing there are several witnesses, the Inspector will be compelled to admit that it actually happened—and that will greatly help to impress the jury.

'I have already consulted Counsel, Mrs Dawlish, as Mr Beresford requested, and he confirms my view that the best, in fact the only possible defence will be that of insanity. If we once establish that, then much of the unhappy fending and probing of the trial will be avoided. To be most effective, of course, we should have statements from you showing how overtired Mr Dawlish has been lately, and pointing out all possible evidences of overstrain.'

He paused.

'Have you seen my husband?' asked Felicity.

'I am due to see him at five o'clock.'

'When you see him,' said Felicity, 'ask him if he's insane.'

For the first time, she had Osborne at a loss for words. With a few almost perfunctory assurances that he would do his best, the solicitor went out. Ted saw him to the door. As he came back, a clock on the mantelpiece struck four. He glanced out of the window, and said:

'If she's coming, the Ard woman will be here soon.'

'I have a feeling that she'll come,' said Felicity. 'I'll put a kettle on a low gas.' She didn't say a word about Osborne's advice, and Ted ignored it, too. He watched her go into the kitchen, knowing that she was in a mood when she could not sit still.

Then he saw Ruby Ard in the mews; even at a distance she was remarkably like her photograph.

He called softly: 'Fel!'

Felicity came hurrying, and stood by his side in a position from which they could see the other woman without at first being seen. Ruby Ard was walking from the entrance of the mews, with long, brisk strides. She was dressed in a cotton suit, pale blue with huge black spots. Ted knew that she had been with the police for several hours that morning, but they had not detained her. Ted had sent her a message, while she had been at the Yard.

Ruby drew nearer.

Felicity said: 'She's like I was, fifteen years ago.'

Ted grunted, but did not say that he agreed, that this was a woman who would attract Dawlish, and that was what Felicity had meant. The visitor came so briskly, and without the slightest hesitation, glanced up at the number on the door of the flat, and then came up the steps.

The front-door bell rang.

'I'll answer it,' said Ted, and lumbered off.

Felicity stood trying to be detached, trying not to think beyond the fact that Pat had said two people might help, one now dead, and this fresh-eyed, clean-limbed, wholesome-looking woman. Ruby Ard had a nice speaking voice; that was evident as she spoke to Ted. His voice rumbled. Felicity reminded herself that the woman might take any attitude; that she had almost certainly told the police that Dawlish had forced her to let him stay at the flat.

She came in.

They stood and looked at each other for a moment, and then Ruby moved forward, with her right hand outstretched, and said:

'I can understand why he wasn't even slightly interested in me, Mrs Dawlish.'

Felicity found herself holding the other's hands, and being completely disarmed.

'It's very good of you to come.'

'It isn't at all,' said Ruby, 'it's the least I can do. I don't know how much you know, Mrs Dawlish, but your husband—may I call him Pat?—spent all of a day and a night in my one room, and if I'm sure of anything in this world, I'm sure he's quite innocent.'

What a boon she was, already.

'He was absolutely up against it, and hated the need for staying in hiding,' Ruby went on, 'and I just don't believe he could have put up an act. As soon as the police allowed me to go, I hurried here.'

'At least they did let you go,' said Felicity, because it was something to say, and she could not quite control her voice.

Ruby smiled, in that restrained and attractive way of hers.

'There was a time when I thought they wouldn't, but I did manage to persuade them that although I sheltered Pat, I wasn't really an accessory after any murder. Pat did suggest that I should tell them that he'd scared me into letting him stay, but—well, the truth sounded much more convincing.' Ruby raised her hands as if she was putting something aside. 'How can I help, Mrs Dawlish?' Her eyes were very bright indeed. 'That's all I want to do.'

On that instant, a new thought came into Felicity's mind.

'I don't trust her,' she told herself.

'It did look as if the situation was as black as it could be,' went on Ruby, matter-of-factly, 'but after Hillman—' she broke off.

'Hillman's death could be called manslaughter, as it was in a fight, and Hillman was armed,' put in Ted. 'It might even be self-defence—there's no evidence that Dawlish tried to kill him, only that he meant to shoot Dawlish. The woman's made that clear, and I've checked with our solicitor. We needn't worry too much about the death of Hillman, except—'

'He can't tell the truth, so he can't help,' Ruby said briskly. 'But *some*one must be able to. Who else was at the Pack of Lies last night?' She moved to a chair and sat on the arm, and began to pull off a glove. 'I hate to admit it, but I told Pat where he would find Hillman. I'd traced Hillman there. If I'd only kept my mouth shut.'

'She's telling the truth, but I simply don't trust her,' Felicity warned herself again, and felt a kind of excitement.

'Can you get at anyone else who was at the Pack of Lies?' asked Ruby. 'Perhaps the woman.'

'Not easily,' Ted answered, and seemed to wake up. He had been staring at her intently. 'The police have had a go at all the people there—the barmen, a barmaid, and the manager and his wife. I went round this morning, but it's closed,' he went on. 'Not surprising. I did ask a few people, and picked up one or two little things.'

'What?' asked Ruby, quickly.

'You didn't tell me,' Felicity said.

'Had to let it sink in,' explained Ted, and ran his fingers through his hair again. 'I saw the barmen having a drink at a pub round the corner. They're all little squirts, all dark-haired, and one has a bald patch.'

Felicity caught her breath.

Ruby said: 'That's like the man Marion said was always following her!'

'That's right,' Ted agreed, woodenly.

'Then you can get at the truth through him—or perhaps his friends.'

'There were four policemen near that pub, all in plain-clothes,' Ted replied, slowly. 'Tim Jeremy and I have had a repu-tation in the past for doing anything we thought might help Pat, and the police haven't given up the idea that we might again. All the barmen are as safe as men can be for the time being. But the police can't keep it up too long.'

'So we've just got to wait,' Ruby said, and looked at Felicity as if with deep compassion. 'I can imagine how awful it must be, but if we can prove that Pat didn't kill Marion or Mrs Wattle, then—'

'Be worth waiting for,' Ted interpolated. 'Miss Ard, what we hoped you'd be able to tell us was whether Pat gave you any information that we haven't got. Whether he found anything out, for instance, at Mrs Wattle's.'

'All he found out was that Hillman had forced Mrs W to say that Marion knew Pat, when she didn't,' declared Ruby. 'He didn't find out another thing. After all, he was only down there for ten minutes or so.'

'I don't trust her,' Felicity seemed to be shouting to herself. 'What is she trying to do?'

Felicity remembered that the kettle was on a low gas. She went into the kitchen, made tea, listened to the other woman talking to Ted, saw the almost spaniel-like look in Ted's eyes when he looked at Ruby Ard, and took in the tea. The other woman did not appear to overdo anything. She was precise in all she said, and positive in her declaration that she was quite sure that Pat had not killed Mrs Wattle.

'And although Marion and I weren't particularly close, we

did meet, and I'm sure that if she'd had a lover, I would have known. Marion was always frightened of men,' Ruby went on, and shook her head as if at some ugly thought. 'That's why I didn't take her seriously about this man who was following her. What I can't understand is, why did he follow her? Why did he try to frighten her? What was he after?'

'You're asking the questions,' Felicity thought, 'and you know the answers.'

Call it intuition, call it whatever she liked, but she felt positive that this woman was quite untrustworthy; that Ruby Ard was involved in these crimes and could save Pat if she told all that she knew, but—what good was intuition? There was not a single fact to work on.

'Mrs Dawlish, I must go now, but I do hope you'll call on me if there's the slightest thing you think I can do,' Ruby said. 'I feel almost as if I shared Pat with you for a day or two, and I don't need telling what a wonderful man he is. Please call on me for anything.'

'I will,' Felicity promised, and tried to infuse some warmth into her voice.

Ruby went off, Ted seeing her to the door. Felicity stood at the window, watching as the other woman walked with long-legged grace towards the square beyond.

Ted came back.

'Well, we struck oil there, Fel, she's just about tops.'

'You fool,' thought Felicity, but could not bring herself to say it; if she told Ted what she thought of Ruby Ard, he would think that her mind was going too.

The other woman's footsteps faded.

'How am I going to make anyone see that she's fooling them?' Felicity found herself asking almost desperately.

Pat hadn't been fooled, he had doubted Ruby. But Ruby Ard was only one of those concerned. She might be involved, but Ted and Tim weren't, and it was almost as if *they* were set in the belief that Pat was guilty. It was as if someone had cast a spell over them.

The telephone bell rang.

It might be a newspaperman; it might be the police; it might be a friend, to say in hushed tones how sorry she was. It could not be Pat, nor anyone likely to be able to help. Felicity felt imprisoned as closely as Pat in his cell at Cannon Row. There was to be a special court, tomorrow morning, when the police would lay their charge formally, and there was no doubt that the hearing would be adjourned, with Pat in custody.

Ted was further from the telephone, so Felicity picked it up.

'Mrs Dawlish speaking.'

'Hallo, Fel,' said a man in a deep and unmistakable voice, and instantly he sent her spirits soaring. 'What have you been doing to the great man?'

'Tim!' Felicity cried. 'Where are you?'

'London Airport,' answered Tim, 'but strictly incognito. The police don't seem interested in me now they've got the big fish. Tell Ted but no one else. What time is the magistrate's court hearing?'

'Half past nine in the morning.'

'Until then I shall lie very low,' declared Tim. 'I would like to make sure my big particular fish can't get away, and if I show my face too soon, they might.'

'What on earth are you talking about?' Ted could see the burning hope in Felicity's eyes as she spoke, the tension in her fingers as she gripped the telephone.

'Just one or two odds and ends that will shatter the police, startle the court, and give you back your hero,' Tim declared. 'I mustn't say more now or I'll have the police on my tail, it's ten to one that they're listening-in. I'll see you in court, that's a promise.'

22

MAGISTRATE'S COURT

Penfold looked into Dawlish's face, his own set and quite without expression, at twenty past nine on the following morning. Dawlish had slept the sleep of the just, had breakfasted well and felt as fit as he had done for a long time, except for his left shoulder and elbow. The shoulder wound had been even less serious than he had thought the day before, and although he could not move his arm, which was in a sling, he felt no pain.

'Good morning, Mr Dawlish.'

'Good morning, Inspector.'

'How is your arm?'

'Much better than Hillman meant it to be.'

'You are aware that you are about to appear before the magistrate, aren't you?'

'Yes.' Dawlish was also aware that he was caught as fast as a man in a vice.

'I would like to remind you again that all we want, all I want, is to get at the truth.'

'Very touching,' murmured Dawlish, and he smiled. 'And

mutually agreeable, too. Have you checked on that bald-headed boy who was probably at the Pack of Lies?'

'Everything necessary is being done,' Penfold said, then came to the real point of his homily. 'It will serve no purpose if you attempt to escape on the way to the court, Mr Dawlish.'

'Good lord!' exclaimed Dawlish. 'I hadn't even thought of it! I'm not slipping, I've slipped.'

One of the men with Penfold smothered a grin.

That helped, a little.

Dawlish was led out of the Cannon Row Police Station to a waiting car. In all, six men were close to him. Outside the gates were twenty photographers, and they all seemed to snap him at once. Two or three called out. A woman shouted: 'Why don't they hang the devil?' Dawlish bent down and got into the big car, still smiling; for Penfold, for the photographers, for the whole wide world. But he had never felt less like smiling, never felt so despairing. He had seen the newspapers and had read every account, and it was impossible to blame Penfold for thinking him guilty. The framing had been done with an infinite cunning; and he still did not know by whom.

He had tried desperately, since waking, to pick out something from what had happened to show a pointer, and there was only one.

Ruby Ard had told him about the Pack of Lies; so Ruby Ard had lured him there. Was 'lured' the right word? He had gone over their conversation time and time again. She had volunteered the information, had given what had appeared to be a good explanation of how she had come to know, but—would a man like Hillman let himself be fooled by the sister of a girl he had almost certainly murdered?

If he were free, Dawlish would work on that, would examine and concentrate only on Marion's sister.

Would Ted?
Would Tim, if he came back?
Where was Tim, and why had he run away?

The court was crowded as it was only on great occasions. The magistrate sat in solitary state, his solemn clerk beneath him, and it seemed that they were the only people, except Dawlish, who really had room to move. There were a hundred people in a public gallery made for fifty. The Press benches were jammed tight so that no one had elbow room, and behind each sitting reporter, one was standing.

Dawlish stood in the dock.

Felicity was at the front of the public benches, with Ted by her side. Felicity had waved a hand, and was smiling at him. She looked lovely, and even looked radiant; she would do, if only to make it obvious that she still believed in him. Ted was his burly self, and kept looking about the courtroom; uneasily? Ruby Ard was near the back of the public seats, looking calm and competent. Osborne was sitting with three other solicitors, very close to Dawlish. Very few Scotland Yard men were actually in court, but Penfold was taking the oath. Behind Dawlish were four policemen, there to create a solid wall of resistance if he did try to run for it. And there were three times the usual number of uniformed police present.

'. . . help me God,' Penfold finished.

The charge was Mrs Wattle's murder, and Penfold was very precise and formal, giving first evidence of the reasons for the charge, then evidence of arrest; he took four minutes. Osborne was watching him closely all the time, and not looking at Dawlish. To Dawlish, it was mumbo-jumbo. He kept glancing at Felicity, and now Felicity had caught Ted's habit, and was peering about the court as if seeking someone who wasn't there. They kept staring at the three doors which led into it, too.

People squeezed in; no one squeezed out.

The magistrate said: 'Thank you, Inspector,' and looked at Dawlish. He was a middle-aged man, severe-faced, clean-shaven, thin-haired, and he was dressed in black. 'Is the accused represented?'

'If you please, your honour,' said Osborne, and stood up slowly. In court, he was rather too formal, and he looked quite small. Obviously he wanted to be the centre of attraction, he rustled papers importantly, studied Dawlish, then the magistrate, and finally Penfold.

'I am appearing on behalf—' he began.

Dawlish saw Felicity's face light up, and that was quite unbelievable.

Ted's did, too; which made it quite crazy.

Dawlish forgot Osborne and the magistrate, and stared towards the door from which the public entered. Tim Jeremy appeared, tall and thin, angular, so burned with the sun that he looked almost like a coloured man; and his grey eyes flashed across the small courtroom. He placed the tips of the thumb and forefinger of his right hand together, and shook his hand at Dawlish.

Osborne was saying:

'. . . so if it please your honour, I would like to make it clear that my client has a complete answer to this charge, but that in the circumstances he does not think it fit to waste the court's time by asking for bail. He is confident, and I am confident, that eight days from now the court will be given a complete and fully established case showing why the charge should be dismissed.'

Tim said, very clearly: 'Why wait until then?'

The magistrate's clerk looked round, shocked. The magistrate pretended not to notice, but glanced up under his eyebrows. Osborne swung round. Two large policemen closed upon Tim, who was at the back of the crowd.

The magistrate said to Osborne: 'Are you calling any witnesses at this stage, Mr Osborne?'

'No, sir, I need time—'

'May I call a witness, your worship?' asked Dawlish. He kept a straight face, but his heart was pounding, for Tim would not make an interruption like this unless he were absolutely sure of himself.

'Really, I am entrusted with the defence of my client, and I cannot—' began Osborne.

'If the accused would like to call a witness against your advice, perhaps you would like a short recession to discuss the matter with him,' suggested the magistrate.

Penfold and the police solicitor did not speak or whisper to one another. Osborne gulped, looked at Dawlish, then turned and stared at Tim, who was now at the front of the public gallery, flanked by two policemen. Ruby looked round from her seat. Thirty people, all standing and packed very tightly, were between her and the door. Ruby stood up, then sat down again.

The magistrate said: 'Are you positive that you have evidence which will influence the court?'

'Yes, your honour,' answered Tim. 'Beyond a shadow of doubt.'

'Very well, you may go into the box.'

'Thank you, your honour.'

There was no sound except that of his footsteps as Tim crossed the court and stepped into the witness-box. He picked up the Bible, and took the oath; then the magistrate adjusted his horn-rimmed glasses and said:

'You may make your statement, Mr Jeremy.'

'Thank you, sir,' Tim said briskly. 'I have just returned from Andalusia, in Southern Spain, where I have been making inquiries on behalf of the accused relating to the murder of Miss Marion Ard—'

'You are aware, I trust, that we are concerned only with the death of Mrs Wattle?'

'Yes, your honour,' said Tim, who looked as if he could hardly restrain himself, he was so delighted. 'I am sure that you will agree that my statement is wholly relevant. I discovered that Miss Marion Ard was to inherit from a maternal Spanish uncle—a man of eighty-seven years of age and expected to die within the next few months—a sum not of fifteen thousand but of approximately one hundred and seven thousand pounds, together with certain potentially valuable mineral rights on land in Andalusia. I also discovered that this inheritance had been represented as being of comparatively little value, and that Marion Ard did not know there was any substantial sum involved and did not know that she was to be the main beneficiary. I also discovered that Miss Marion Ard had been represented in Spain by Mr Osborne, who is in this court now, and that Mr Osborne withheld from his client important information about this inheritance.'

Osborne was on his feet. His quiet, precise voice wilted, he stammered twice, and passed his hand across his forehead, then burst out:

'Your honour, this is ridiculous! There is not a word of truth in what this man says.'

His eyes were glittering as he stared at Tim.

'I have positive proof, your honour,' Tim said, quite as jubilant a schoolboy as Penfold could ever be. And Penfold watched, open-mouthed. 'What is more, I also have proof that Mr Osborne and Ruby, the sister of Marion Ard, met on several occasions in the small town of Arona, in Spain, and in fact lived at hotels in various small Andalusian towns as man and wife. I further—'

Osborne was looking about him as if in horror and disbelief. Penfold was staring at him, and a uniformed policeman was very close to his side.

'Tim,' Dawlish was thinking, chokily, 'bless your great heart, Tim.' He felt as if his legs would not hold him, and gripped the dock rail with his sound hand. Felicity was leaning forward, staring at Tim as if every word he uttered was worth a million pounds.

Penfold had started to turn red.

Ted was glancing round at Ruby Ard, who was trying to get to the exit. All her colour and poise had gone, she was trembling. A policeman was standing straight in front of the door, with a hand on the handle, and she stood staring at him, then spun round towards Osborne.

He was looking as if he wished part of the wall or the floor would open to swallow him up.

Penfold was muttering as if to himself.

'It was Osborne who sold me the idea that I ought to run away, so that I couldn't be compelled to give evidence against Pat,' went on Tim, and all formality dropped away from him; he actually grinned. 'Osborne spoon-fed me with the evidence he said the police had accumulated against Pat. Taken at its face value it was nasty, but I've met Pat Dawlish before. And I wondered why Osborne was anxious to get me out of the country.'

Osborne now stood with his hands clenched by his sides, the only colour in his glittering eyes; he *looked* like a murderer.

Ruby was actually in front of the policeman, who put a hand on her arm. She tried to push past him, but he stopped her.

The magistrate's clerk whispered earnestly, the magistrate had a hand in front of his mouth, as if to hide a smile. The police solicitor was on his feet, saying: 'If it please your honour,' time and time again. Osborne stood rigid in the well of the court, while Ruby stood by the constable, who refused to let her leave.

'. . . Osborne was so anxious to send me out of the country,' Tim repeated. 'Funny thing happened, too. I knew there was a Spanish angle to this business, and on Osborne's brief-case when I first saw him I saw a hotel label from the town of Cueva, in Andalusia. It started me thinking. So I got hold of photographs of him and Ruby Ard—from a newspaper file—and went off to hide, as he thought. I got myself a Spanish *visa* at Perpignan, and bob's your—'

The magistrate banged his gavel.

'The court is adjourned,' he announced, and his clerk looked enormously relieved.

Felicity was on her feet, and a policeman helped her over the rail towards the dock. No one stopped her from taking Dawlish's right hand; and no one now held back Tim and Ted. But two policemen were very close to Osborne, and another had his hand on Ruby's arm so that she could not run away.

Penfold arrived, still red, very solemn, and with a shocked look in his eyes; but he kept his poise remarkably well.

'I want to see all of you about this,' he said. 'You first, Mr Jeremy, please.'

'If it please your honour,' said the solicitor for the police, an hour later, 'I have been instructed to withdraw the charge against Patrick Dawlish, with your permission, and to state that charges will be preferred against other individuals at an early date.'

'Mr Dawlish,' said the magistrate, smiling quite openly, 'the charge is withdrawn and you are quite free to go.'

23

TIM

'Now don't crowd me,' Tim protested, in the front room of the mews flat. 'I've had to fight about a million newspaper johnnies, not to mention a few odd millions of the Great British Public, so as to get here. The mews is like a film première with Marilyn Monroe up.' He brushed his straight hair back from his forehead, and his eyes showed up vivid against his dark tan. 'I'm more sunburned than you are, Pat. Did you two stay canoodling in your cabin all day?'

'Don't hold out on us,' Ted ordered.

Dawlish was sitting in the largest armchair, with Felicity on its arm, her hand at the back of Dawlish's head.

'All right, all right,' said Tim, and sipped a whisky and soda. 'I really gave you the gen in court. The thing that first puzzled me was Osborne's habit of showing how bad the case was against you. Knowing the strength of the enemy is one thing, but you don't have to keep hitting yourself with it. He'd been Marion Ard's solicitor and I knew she'd asked him for help—he actually told me so when I went to see him about her, the day you sailed, Pat. He was all pro-Patrick and eager to help, and seemed on top of his job. He said that since the disappearance of Marion Ard he'd had private inquiry agents checking you, to see if there was any possibility of an association—and there was. Then I faced this fact that when Fel was ill, you nearly went off your rocker. I knew you really did, up to a point, but Osborne made it sound ten times worse. So I started looking round a bit, and discovered that he'd been to Spain once or twice, as I told you. Things then began to jell.'

Tim sipped his drink again, before going on:

'Made another discovery, too. Osborne had been known to slip into the Pack of Lies for a quick one, but it wasn't really on his beat. One of the barmen measured up to the description of the chap always chasing Marion, too—I couldn't swear he was the same fellow, but he looked it. I wanted more definite evidence, as Penfold was after your scalp, and the odds did look heavy.'

'Not much doubt what the devils tried at first,' interposed Ted, heavily. 'They tried to drive Marion Ard off her head, or into committing suicide. Then she wouldn't take no from you, Pat, and that created a new situation.'

Dawlish said dryly. 'New is one word.'

Felicity was playing with his thick, fair hair.

'I don't suppose we'll ever know exactly what happened after you'd left for Southampton,' Tim put in, 'but it's obvious that they killed Marion so that murder was unmistakable. Obviously Osborne or Ruby hatched up the idea of fixing it on to you. You would be a potential source of danger when you got back and found that she'd been murdered, for you would almost certainly start investigating. Osborne didn't like the idea, having heard of your reputation, and the rest followed logically.

'Once it was under way, it was Patrick Dawlish or Mr Ruddy Osborne, and he didn't intend it to be him,' Tim added. 'Through

Hillman, who used to work at the Pack of Lies, Osborne had forced Mrs Wattle to lie about you and Marion Ard. So Mrs Wattle was the one weak link. She made a habit of petty pilfering from the tenants, and we now know that twice she robbed a tenant who had died at the house. Hillman still had that hold on her, but she remained a weak link, and would probably crack if our Patrick got at her.

'We now know what happened the night he did see her,' Tim went on, 'and how Hillman took his chance to silence a witness and frame Pat again. Quick work, wasn't it? Later, when you left Harven Street, Ruby Ard telephoned Hillman, who was all ready to receive you.'

Felicity's hand stopped for a moment.

'The woman at the pub's admitted that he had a telephone call just before you arrived,' Tim declared.

'How did you get all this, Tim?' asked Felicity.

'Bit of two-ing and two-ing, plus a few confidences from Penfold,' Tim said. 'That chap can't say he's sorry often enough. Tell you another thing, Pat. You were a great danger to the Osborne-Ruby set up from the moment Marion came to see you. They didn't know what she had suspected and told you, you see, and they had to find out what you knew. That was why Ruby went to Four Ways, disarming you by admitting she was also a suspect. She is the most effective liar I know, and managed it by telling the simple truth,' added Tim, with great feeling. 'She had you in her room long enough to feel sure you didn't suspect her or Osborne, and after that it was just a question of making sure you were caught.'

'What I want to know is, why did you go off making me think you thought Pat was guilty?' Ted demanded.

'Simple, Ted. You had to look as worried as a bloodhound put on a murderer's trail and picking up his master's scent, so as to make Osborne feel absolutely secure. I can tell you now, thanks to Penfold, that Hillman and another barman took Marion's body to Four Ways, one night just after you'd gone. Another odd thing: Marion did suspect her sister—Ruby admits that—and Penfold thinks she wouldn't ask the Yard for help because of that. But so as to get his help, she told Pat that she had tried to. Penfold is busy hunting for excuses for his lapses, you see.'

'I'll bloodhound you,' Ted growled, belatedly.

'Why didn't you telephone from Spain?' Felicity asked, almost idly.

'My dear sweet Fel, these people were cold-blooded killers. All I discovered I wanted to keep to myself until I could use it to the fullest effect. Had Pat still been free and on the run, I might have taken a chance and tried to persuade Penfold by telephone that I'd got at the truth, but by the time I had the evidence I needed, Pat was under arrest. And I always did resent the fact that his ugly mug invariably gets in the newspapers, this time I'll bet it's mine.'

'I ought to break your neck,' Ted said. 'But I won't.'

'Seventeen different photographs of Tim, fourteen of you, seven of me and four of Ted,' announced Felicity, next morning, 'and eighteen of Ruby Ard and Osborne!' She put down the newspapers, last night's and this morning's, which had been delivered by a newsagent told to bring 'the lot'. 'Tim ought to be satisfied,' she went on. 'Darling, had you the faintest idea that Osborne was involved?'

'Not a suspicion. I wasn't sure about Ruby Ard. I'd seen the Pack of Lies angle as a bait, but Osborne and the big inheritance—no.'

'The amazing thing is that for a while Ted actually believed you'd done it,' Felicity said. 'There were times when I could have kicked him. I didn't think the time would ever come when I'd almost hate the sight of him and the thought of Tim. I really did think that Tim had run off because he thought you were guilty, too.'

'Which makes it fifty-fifty,' said Dawlish. 'Queer thing. Ted, Tim and I would trust one another with just about everything, yet under real stresses, big doubts creep in. Tim and Ted of me, me of Tim and Ted.' He eased his position in the armchair. 'Which makes you one in four hundred million,' he went on. 'The one who didn't doubt me.'

'Didn't I?' asked Felicity, of herself.

'Don't be silly,' she said roundly, 'there wasn't the slightest doubt. Darling, how's your shoulder?'

'It'll be all right in a week or so.'

'You won't be able to do much with the pigs or the trees yet, will you?'

Dawlish looked at her suspiciously.

'Now what?'

'I wondered if you'd like a week or two's holiday-cum-convalescence,' Felicity suggested, blandly.

'I would,' said Dawlish. 'Right here, at Four Ways, Alum, in the county of Surrey, England. I mean to make sure that no one tries to hide another body.'

About the Author

John Creasey, born in 1908, was a paramount English crime and science fiction writer who used myriad pseudonyms for more than six hundred novels. He founded the UK Crime Writers' Association in 1953. In 1962, his book *Gideon's Fire* received the Edgar Award for Best Novel from the Mystery Writers of America. Many of the characters featured in Creasey's titles became popular, including George Gideon of Scotland Yard, who was the basis for a subsequent television series and film. Creasey died in Salisbury, UK, in 1973.

THE PATRICK DAWLISH MYSTERIES

FROM OPEN ROAD MEDIA

OPEN ROAD

INTEGRATED MEDIA

INTEGRATED MEDIA

Find a full list of our authors and
titles at www.openroadmedia.com

FOLLOW US
@OpenRoadMedia